For Hudson, Aspen and Landon

For further information, contact:
Tumblehome, Inc.
201 Newbury St, Suite 201
Boston, MA 02116
http://tumblehomebooks.org/

Library of Congress Control Number 2019902556
ISBN-13 978-1-943431-48-9
ISBN-10 1-943431-48-5

Pell, Eva J.
ResQ and the Baby Orangutan / Eva J. Pell - 1st ed
Illustrated by Mattias Lanas
Borneo map (page 14) credit: https://commons.wikimedia.org/wiki/File:Borneo2_map_english_names.svg
Mortadelo2005 [CC BY-SA 3.0 (http://creativecommons.org/licenses/by-sa/3.0/)] (modified)

Printed in Taiwan

10 9 8 7 6 5 4 3 2 1

ResQ AND THE BABY ORANGUTAN

SAVING ONE ANIMAL AT A TIME

Eva J. Pell
Illustrated by Mattias Lanas

TUMBLEHOME, Inc.

CONTENT

1.   STUCK IN THE PINE BARRENS

From the bank of the pond I see my cousin Stowe, waist deep in a sphagnum bog, her arms flailing.

"Help, I'm stuck. Get me out of here," she yells.

"What are you doing?" I holler back. "We're supposed to be getting ready for a mission in Indonesia, not taking a mud bath."

"Sorry, Wheaton. While you were checking out the equipment, I wanted to sneak a look at some pitcher plants. The Pine Barrens have tons of them. I had to creep out on this bog to get the perfect picture." She points to a weird-looking plant, kind of a miniature purple horn of plenty. "I got a photo, but then I fell through. Give me your hand, and I'll yank myself out of here."

Will be interesting to see how this works. Stowe is twelve, a year older than me, and a whole head taller. At least she's skinny.

What a maneuver. Stowe tosses her cell phone up onto dry land first, and holds onto me while she slithers out of the bog onto firm ground. How I stay out of the pond is a miracle.

I look at Stowe's legs, caked in mud. "Yuck. No way are you getting into one of my space suits with that muck on you."

"Well, at least I got an awesome shot of an insect trapped in the pitcher plant." She opens up the picture on her cell phone to show me.

"Wow. That's crazy." I would say more but my cell phone is buzzing. Looks like I missed a bunch of texts.

"WHERE ARE YOU? I KEEP TEXTING BUT YOU DON'T ANSWER."

Uh oh. That would be my grandmother, Ariella. The message feels like a laser hitting my pocket. Surprised my pants don't have holes in them. Much as I don't relish a conversation, this is going to take more than a text. I give her a call, and she picks up on the first ring.

"Wheaton, what's with this note you left me about a job for **ResQ** in Indonesia?" My grandmother doesn't even take time to say hello first. "And you're out at the base?"

I wait a second to be sure Ariella has finished, and put the phone on speaker so Stowe can listen in.

"Stowe and I were hanging at the house playing cards. A call came in from Angga Rezaputra, a park ranger at

Gunung Palung National Park in Indonesia. He said that they found a mother orangutan with a bullet wound to one of her front arms—"

"We're not a police service," Ariella interrupts.

"I know. I'm getting to the rescue part. This female, Bella, has a baby, who's around one. And the little guy, he goes by Buddi, is missing—may have been poached. Angga saw our new ResQ website, and how we're the Emergency Service for the Rescue of Endangered Species. He locked on to the part about us having tools to help find missing animals. He said he was super short of staff because they all went off to do some training thing. He pushed hard for us to come help. I had to say yes."

"You didn't think you should check with me first?"

"I tried to call, but you left your cell phone in the kitchen when you went for a bike ride."

"Wheaton, your parents agreed to let you stay with me for a while, and maybe come on a rescue close by for starters. Not sure they'll go along with a mission halfway around the world."

Ariella seems to have ignored my explanation, but she knows my mother, her daughter, who can hover with the best of the helicopters.

"Mom was worried until I reminded her that we've had shots for every disease in creation. Besides, it was my parents' idea for me to take a break after finishing college so I can spend time with you, learning about the world outside the engineering lab."

"And what about your cousin? We can't just leave her

and run off to Indonesia after she's come down to visit for spring break."

"I know. That's why she has to join us. Stowe knows everything about the natural world, I mean, not as much as you, but almost."

Stowe pipes in, "Please Grandma, don't send me home. I can't miss out on the adventure. And I've read so much about orangutans. It'll be so cool to see some in person."

"Have you checked this out with your folks? Don't assume because you're home-schooled, you can go off to Indonesia without asking."

"Oh, I know. I talked to my mother and she's fine with me going. Spring has come early back home. The snow's turned to an icy slush, and ski practice was cancelled. She did say I have to keep logs on everything, so I don't slip in my schoolwork."

Neither one of us bothers to mention that both moms said we needed to check with our grandmother first. And we didn't tell our parents that there might be poachers involved.

"Wheaton, is the **ECAPS** fueled up for the trip around the world? And have you checked to be sure the **HeliBoaJee** is in good working order? I'm guessing we'll need to use it in all three modes – **Heli**copter, **Boat** and **Jee**p." Our grandmother likes to be prepared.

"All our vehicles are in great shape. Trust me. The ECAPS is ready to blast off. It's been sunny, so the solar cells have generated all the hydrogen we need. The methane fuel tanks are full too, thanks to a recent garbage dump, and I have the powdered aluminum stashed for our return fuel."

"And do you have all the gear we need for the rescue?"

"Before we biked out here, we packed and loaded everything in your car. But most important, we need you and your cameras," I add. Yeah, I'm sucking up, but our grandmother is a famous wildlife photographer, and she does want to document all our rescues.

Stowe and I look at each other, fingers crossed. There's a pretty long silence, and I wonder if we've lost cell phone connection.

"I will agree to go," Ariella says, "with one condition. We can assist in locating this missing baby orangutan, but our work needs to be at a distance. Under no circumstances is ResQ to be in direct contact with any poachers. These people can be dangerous. Understood?"

"Got it," we say in unison.

"All right then. I'll get my stuff together and see you soon."

The two of us bump fists, then elbows, and twirl around, just like we've been doing since we were old enough to stand.

"We'll be waiting for you on the tarmac next to Hangar #36. Bye."

I hang up before Ariella has time to change her mind.

2. Preparing For Rescue

As I say goodbye to my grandmother, I remember my mud-encrusted cousin. "Stowe, you better get back to our hangar and clean yourself up before Ariella gets here. There's a bathroom you can use, right inside the door. Oh, and best to keep this soggy boggy adventure to ourselves."

"Got it," she says as she races off.

I follow, walking down Hangar Road inside the McGuire-Dix-Lakehurst military base. A jeep passes me, and the driver gives me a wave. A while back, Ariella introduced me to an Air Force lieutenant colonel in charge of technology development. She got interested in the inventions I'm developing for ResQ and invited me to work with one of her teams on some special projects. I do get paid, but she also gives us space to store our vehicles.

When I get back to the hangar, Stowe is waiting for me, all cleaned up, wearing a t-shirt with a logo that says *Endless Winter*. Interesting choice for a trip to the tropics.

Before I can comment on her wardrobe, my cell phone buzzes.

"ALL PACKED UP. LEAVING NOW. BE AT THE BASE SOON."

"Ariella's on her way," I tell Stowe.

"Is there time for you to show me the ECAPS and all that stuff you guys were discussing before?"

"Sure. Follow me."

As we walk into the hangar, Stowe gives me a funny look. "I've been meaning to ask you, when did you start calling Grandma, Ariella?"

"Since we've gone into the rescue business together."

"Hmm. Should I call her that too?"

"Why not, it's her name?"

"I know. It seems a little weird..."

Stowe gets distracted as she focuses on a picture sitting on my work table. "Our last family photo with Great Grandpa Gordino." She reaches out and touches the image of his face.

"Yeah. Grandma thought we should keep his picture here, at least until we have real headquarters." Our great grandfather died about a year ago. He owned a chain of pizza stores, but, like his daughter, his real love was wildlife. When he got sick, GG told Ariella that when he was gone she should sell the stores and start ResQ.

Stowe blows GG a kiss and then runs into the high bay area. "What on earth is that strange thing? Looks like a giant upside-down ice cream cone."

"That, Cuz, is the ECAPS, our personal mini-space shuttle. At a speed of 17,500 miles per hour, it'll get us where we need to go super fast."

"Whoa, Genius Boy, I had no idea you were building something like this! And you mean that solar wall really fuels this thing?" Stowe asks.

"Yup." I ignore the "Genius Boy" part. Stowe usually spares me that kind of comment. "The hydrogen I use as jet propulsion fuel is produced by splitting water using the energy from the sun. You are feasting your eyes on the backside of an array of tiny, three-dimensional solar panels."

"And can you really make enough hydrogen to get the ECAPS launched? We tried solar power at our house in Vermont. We ended up in the dark a lot of the time."

"This is Wheaton-designed technology. And we have a lot more sun in New Jersey, in case you missed it. But don't worry. I have a backup fuel if it's cloudy."

"All right, oh brilliant one," Stowe says, throwing up her hands. "And you call this marvel ECAPS because that's SPACE spelled backwards?"

"Good catch, puzzle queen."

Stowe starts to move on and then stops in her tracks. "So we're really going up into space in that thing?" She takes a deep breath and gives me a half grin. "I guess I'm in your hands."

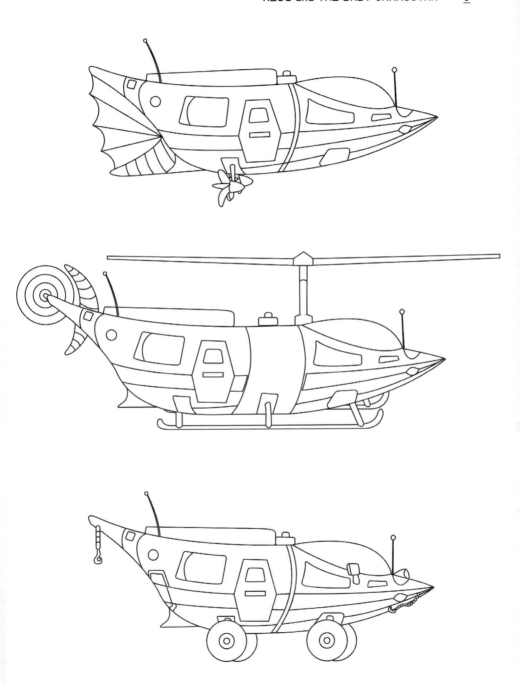

Stowe's nervousness seems to evaporate as she wanders over to another vehicle based on one of my designs.

"Is this that *Heebeejeebee* Grandma referred to?"

"Yup, that's my HeliBoaJee. It is the ultimate convertible —Helicopter, speed-Boat and Jeep—"

"I get it, like the Swiss army knife of all-terrain vehicles," she interrupts.

The tour is cut short as we hear a car door slam.

Stowe races out ahead of me. "Hi, Grandma," she says. "I'm so excited to be going with you and Wheaton on this rescue."

Ariella smiles at us, and then points a finger at me. "We're not going quite yet. I need some details from you kids."

"Like I said, we have to get to Gunung Palung National Park in Indonesia to rescue a baby orangutan."

"And where, to be precise, is this park? You do understand that Indonesia is made of 18,000 islands? Orangutans are found on Borneo and Sumatra. Which island is the park on? Where do we land? Will Angga be meeting us?"

I guess I am short on details. Rather than make eye contact, I text Angga with the relevant questions. Lucky for me he answers before the interrogation can continue.

"Okay," I say without looking up. "We're headed to Borneo. Angga suggests we land at Ketapang Airport, a small airstrip on the west coast. He'll let the authorities know we're coming. They'll give us a place to stash the ECAPS away from snooping eyes. From there we take the HeliBoa-Jee to the park. He'll text more instructions when we land."

Ariella points to the hangar. "Let's get our gear stowed for the trip. It's 4:00 PM here in New Jersey and 4:00 AM tomorrow in Borneo—"

"Yikes. It's 4:00 AM? I forgot about the time change. Must have woken Angga up. I hope he won't be irritated with me before we even get there."

Ariella arches her eyebrows and continues. "If we get going soon, we should land around sunrise. That'll give us a head start searching."

I hand Stowe a headset with a built-in microphone. "This will be helpful for writing your logs. I designed it for keeping records during our rescues. It converts what you say into grammatically correct and spell-checked paragraphs. And there's a feature that does Google searches for extra information. You can download your files to a computer later."

"Awesome. My logs will be perfect!" Stowe gives me a thumbs up as she positions the headset on top of her tangle of yellow curls.

Ariella drives the HeliBoaJee up the ramp into the ECAPS. Once it's locked in place, we go to load the rest of our gear. I point to one box marked fragile. "This is the **Finder**, my latest invention. I'll explain more about it when we get to Borneo."

"So mysterious." My cousin gives me a wink.

With everything stored on board, I hand my companions helmets and shiny blue space suits we'll wear for the flight.

"So cool, my favorite color!" Stowe says. "They don't look anything like those robot suits you see in the Smithsonian Air and Space Museum in D.C."

"Correct, these are the latest model. They're designed to fit almost like a second skin. Turn on your sleeve computer. As we travel into space, it'll adjust the pressure so you won't self-destruct."

"That's reassuring," Stowe says with a dramatic shudder.

To get the ECAPS to the launch pad, I send a signal that lifts the spaceship onto a pair of rails. We open the high bay door and send the ship down to one of the runways on the base where we can launch clear of any trees. Another command from me positions it for lift-off.

We climb a ladder, flip open a small door above us, and squeeze into a tight compartment at the tip of the spacecraft. I sit down in the pilot seat. Stowe plops down beside me in the co-pilot chair.

Ariella peers down at Stowe. "You're in my spot, Missy."

"But I'm the navigator."

"You can do your job from back there." Ariella points to a seat behind me. The navigation system is mounted on a gooseneck, like a lamp. Ariella bends it back into Stowe's lap as she sits down and straps herself in.

Our grandmother slides in next to me. She's so tall her knees are up near her chin. At least we won't be in here too long.

I crane my head back in Stowe's direction. "Could you send a quick text to our parents and let them know we're headed out? I did promise my mom we'd check in before leaving. Your mom's always so cool, but might as well let her know too." Texting—the perfect form of communication. Provides information without the need for conversation.

"Done," Stowe reports in a flash.

I call into the control tower to confirm the airspace is safe for our takeoff. After double-checking the order for the launch, I take a few deep breaths. Sure don't want Ariella or Stowe to think I'm nervous. But of course Stowe notices.

"Slow your leg down, Wheaton. You're shaking the whole spaceship."

Ariella puts her hand on my shoulder, and my knee stops shaking.

"Everybody ready?" I ask in my most commanding voice.

"Yes," Ariella and Stowe call back.

My cousin is already half in orbit. "Let's get going. This *so* beats doing schoolwork. Feels like I'm about to ski down Mt. Everest."

"Okay guys, count down—10,9,8,7,6,5,4,3,2,1." And with that I yell, "BLAST OFF."

The ECAPS lifts off, streaking through the sky so fast it feels like we're being riveted to the backs of our chairs.

Indonesia is literally on the other side of the world. Stowe, our navigator, sets our course flying west to Borneo.

Borneo

Borneo National Parks

1. Tanjung Puting National Park
(Kalimantan, Indonesian Borneo)
2. Kutai National Park
(East Kalimantan, Indonesian Borneo)
3. Gunung Palung National Park
(West Kalimantan, Indonesian Borneo)
4. Betung Kerihun National Park
(West Kalimantan, Indonesian Borneo)
5. Danum Valley Conservation Area
(Sabah, Malaysian Borneo)

STOWE LEBLOND'S LOG

Pine Barrens, New Jersey

April 10

4:00 PM

We went down to the military base in the Pine Barrens where Wheaton has all his equipment stashed. The base is kind of weird. All these officers running around doing stuff. Wheaton knows a lot of them because of the secret work they do together.

The coolest part of the Pine Barrens is obviously NOT the base, but the woods and wetlands all around. We have sphagnum moss growing along the stream at home in Vermont, but you should see the amount growing along the ponds down here. In some places it's filled in, so its squooshy when you walk on it. And in other spots, it's floating over the water like an anchored raft.

These sphagnum mats are a great place for pitcher plants to grow. Most plants survive by capturing carbon dioxide from the air and converting it into sugars. They get nutrients from the soil or water. Pitcher plants do those things too, but they also eat insects. They get their name because they have these leaves in the shape of a pitcher, maybe eight inches long. The ones here are purple, although I think they come in other colors too. At the top they have a small entrance, looks like a collar. There are small glands that send out nectar, which attract insects. When the hungry bugs start lapping up the nectar, they sometimes slip and _fall down into the pitcher. Guess that's what happens when you're a sloppy eater_ 😊.

Unfortunately for the insects, the "pitcher" is lined with these hairs that bend downward. For the bug, getting out would be like having to walk up a tube against rows and rows of bristles—impossible. If that's not bad enough, there's water at the base of the pitcher (of course, since it's a pitcher), and the bugs can't stay afloat so they drown. And then the plants release enzymes that digest most of the bug – sort of like our stomachs do, I guess. All that's left at the end is the bug's skeleton. No wonder these plants are called carnivorous. I've taken a couple of pictures on my cell phone, including one that shows the insects being captured.

I read there are 32 different types of pitcher plants in Borneo. I'll keep my eyes peeled for them. That's all for now. I have to go.

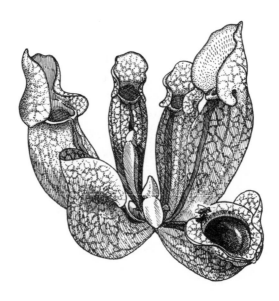

3. ON OUR WAY TO BORNEO

Our little ECAPS is quite the SPACEship. On the ground it may look weird, but once launched, it soars like the best of them.

As I tilt the ECAPS to follow the curvature of the earth, Ariella peers out the window. "Look away from the earth at all the stars out there."

"Wow," Stowe says. "But they're not twinkling."

"Right. On earth the starlight bends a little as it travels through our atmosphere, creating that effect," I explain.

"So if we lived out here no one would ever have written Twinkle, Twinkle Little Star?" Stowe gives my shoulder a little nudge. Then she changes subjects.

"How high up are we?"

"About 400 miles."

"Do we have to worry about being hit by space debris?" I think Stowe's seen too many movies.

"Relax. You're more likely to have something fall off a pickup truck and hit your car on the road, than to be clobbered out here by some random object. There's lots of stuff flying around, but space is, well, space, it's big."

Then I turn my attention to the controls. "Give me a minute to convert us over to the methane fuel for the rest of the trip."

"When you've got that taken care of," Ariella says to me, "maybe we should talk a little about the orangutan we're supposed to be rescuing. Since _you_ accepted this mission, what do you know about these apes?" She's not ready to let me off the hook for leaping into this trip without looking.

"Not much, I guess. They have a whole lot of red hair, and they're smart, right?"

"Really, Wig," Stowe says, messing her hand through my hair, "sounds like you, except for the hair color."

Urggh. So what if I don't waste time getting regular haircuts.

"The two of you need to focus. This flight is only going to last 90 minutes, and since we didn't take the time to prepare, we need to review some things about these animals." Ariella gives me one of those needle nose looks. I'm not making fun of her sharp nose. Well, you get the point.

"Orangutans are very special. They are the only great apes found in Asia, not Africa," Ariella tells us. "Babies are especially precious to orangutans because they only give birth once every seven years. Most animals mate every year.

For them, losing a baby may be very sad. For orangutans who only have four or five in a lifetime, losing babies is a serious threat to species survival."

"Wow, I can see why Angga is so worried," I blurt out.

"If the baby was poached, who's it sold to?" Stowe's asking a great question. "Zoos wouldn't buy those animals, would they?"

"Today no credible zoo would ever take a baby or even a healthy adult from the wild. If you see a baby orangutan in a zoo it was probably born there.

"But poachers don't think twice about selling these babies as pets." Ariella's mouth sags and her eyebrows lift. "Not long ago I saw a very sad picture of a little orangutan in a cage hanging on a wall. It was so thin, and the big bright eyes you see in baby orangutans in the wild were half closed."

I start thinking about my little brother, and what would happen to him if he escaped from my mom. We have to find this baby.

"I know this is a stupid question, but why are these people called poachers and not regular old hunters? Do they like eggs or something?"

"Wheaton, you can be such a dork sometimes."

"Kids!" Ariella's shaking her head at us. "Hard to know why the same word can mean two different things. Poacher is an old word, maybe derived from the French word *poche*, which means pocket. People who trespass and pocket game that is not theirs, are called poachers. And when you poach eggs, the white forms a pocket around the yolk."

"What does it matter?" Stowe's not that interested in word origins. "It's a horrible thing to do."

"Poachers don't eat orangutans, do they?" I hold my stomach at the thought of it.

Ariella takes a breath and sighs. "The poacher's main interest is capturing and selling the babies to make money. This usually means killing the mothers, and because these people are often poor, they will eat her."

"Ughh. Maybe I should become a vegetarian," I say, looking at Stowe.

Stowe gives me a nod, but then focuses on the navigation screen. "We're passing over the equator, heading to Kalimantan, the Indonesian part of Borneo." She gives me the coordinates for Ketapang airport, on the west coast.

On descent, we can see the outline of this huge island. All the cities seem to be along the coast. That must be where most of the roads are located. Good thing we have the Heli-BoaJee so we can travel wherever we want.

The runway stretches in front of us. "Here we go," I say, tilting the ECAPS into its horizontal landing position. A parachute propels out of the back, helping to slow us down. Our full body harnesses hold us back as we touch down on the runway. Ariella's hands grip the arm rests as we jolt to a halt.

A guy in uniform is waiting as we climb out of our craft.

"Are you the group from the USA headed to Gunung Palung National Park?" You can tell this guy is looking at the three of us, not quite believing what he's seeing.

"Yes, I'm **W**heaton **I**van **G**uinto from ResQ, and these are my associates, Ariella Gordon and Stowe LeBlond. We are here to help Ranger Rezaputra at Gunung Palung National Park. Is there a secure hangar where I can park our craft?" I point to the ECAPS and wait for a reaction.

"You flew that thing from the U.S., Mr. Guinto?"

"Yes sir. Not sure how long we'll be here. Need to keep it safe."

The guy looks at me the way most grown-ups do, like I'm a kid who could not possibly know what he's talking about. But after scratching his head, the airport person points down the airstrip. "Go park in the hangar on the end of the runway."

As he walks away, Stowe comes over and puts her arm around me. "My dear associate, while you're moving the

ECAPS, I'll go exchange some dollars for rupiahs and pick up a map."

"Good idea," I say, shaking loose. "Angga did warn me that GPS will be unreliable in some places."

"I assume we can fly up to the park in the HeliBoaJee," Ariella says to me.

"Nope. I just texted Angga, and he said there are storms between here and there. We'll be heading north over land."

STOWE LEBLOND'S LOG

Borneo, Indonesia

April 11

6:30 AM

The trip to Borneo only took 90 minutes thanks to Wheaton's amazing technology. He wants to minimize how much carbon dioxide we put into the atmosphere, since it contributes to global warming. The ECAPS is launched with hydrogen generated by splitting water (H_2O) with the energy from the sun. This happens on a humongous solar wall he created on the side of the hangar.

Once we're in orbit the ECAPS is fueled with methane Wheaton's generated in these giant fuel cells. They're filled with microorganisms that digest garbage and release methane, sort of like cows. I was worried it would smell yucky but Wheaton pointed out that methane is odorless. He told me that hydrogen sulfide, which smells like rotten eggs, is a by-product of the generation process. He assured me that it is removed before the methane is stored. He doesn't like that smell either.

We won't have the solar wall when it's time to come home, so Wheaton's brought along pulverized aluminum. When we need hydrogen for the return flight, he'll put his special mix in water. The aluminum will bind to the oxygen in H_2O, releasing the needed hydrogen fuel. And he got the aluminum powder from recycled soda cans. ResQ is all about minimizing waste!

Borneo is one of the 18,000 islands that make up the country of Indonesia. While as many as 6,000 of the islands are uninhabited, the rest of the islands have lots going on. More than 17 million people live on Borneo along with 15,000 plant species and more than 1,400 amphibians, birds, fish, mammals, reptiles and insects. Indonesia comes right after Brazil in having the most biodiversity in the world.

Borneo is one of the biggest islands in Indonesia and the third biggest island in the world. Mom, in case you're wondering, Greenland and New Guinea are bigger. Borneo is actually only 73% Indonesian. That part is also known as Kalimantan. 26% is part of Malaysia, and 1%, in the North, is the independent country of Brunei.

Borneo is 287,000 square miles in size. Vermont is only 9,623 square miles. That makes Borneo 30 times bigger! Before the last ice age, Borneo was connected to Asia by land bridges. When the ice melted these connections went under water and now Borneo is an island.

I guess a lot changed after the ice age. Borneo's weather is tropical, which is a nice way of saying hot and humid. I guess that's because the equator runs right through the island. The park we are going to, Gunung Palung, is less than 100 miles south of the equator! We are going to the middle of the earth, sort of ☺. The wet season is from November to March, and what they call the dry season is from April through October. Not sure that there is anything close to dry in a place that averages 150 inches of rain a year. In Vermont we have an average of 36 inches of rain per year.

We do get 81 inches of snow on average, but at least you can ski on it!

I'm excited to see this island. Looks like most of the people live along the coasts, some of which are pretty swampy. There are some tall mountains and many rivers. Most of the rivers are only navigable for around 100 miles, which means any boat that tries to go farther is going to end up lost or stuck. That's why so much of Borneo is still a mystery. Good thing we have the HeliBoaJee to help us get around. And, of course, I'm a great navigator.

4. What's For Breakfast?

S towe has rejoined us with money and a map.

"We're ready to go." I point to the HeliBoaJee. "There's plenty of methane to get us to the park. Where we're going there are loads of peat swamps, which give off tons of methane. I have a concentrator to refuel the Heli-BoaJee pretty much anywhere there's a bog."

"Cool. Maybe we can see some more pitcher plants." Stowe gives me an elbow.

Then she changes the subject. "There's one thing we forgot to bring..."

"No way we are flying back to New Jersey."

"Don't flip your wig, Wig. We need to pick up some food before heading to the park. It's the beginning of the day, and we're going to get hungry." As usual, food is at the top of Stowe's list of worries.

"Good idea," Ariella says, looking over the map. "The next leg of our trip will take a while. It's about 65 miles to Teluk Melano from here, and depending on the roads, it could be slow going. Let's convert the HeliBoaJee into jeep mode and find someplace to buy something to eat before we leave town."

I retract the rotor blades and landing skids as the wheels lock into place. Driving away from the airport heading north, we see a local market and cafe.

The three of us go in and look around. Not much looks familiar. Metal racks are piled high with rice and spices. There's a familiar smell that reminds me of the international grocery store near my family's apartment building in Hoboken, New Jersey. And row after row of food with labels we can't understand. I sure wish we'd packed more candy bars.

Stowe walks over to the place I guess you'd call their take-out section. "Looks like there's something we can buy here called *nasi campur*." She reads the name on the sign in the food case. "It's a platter with some sort of rice and helpings of meat, vegetables, tofu and beans. I guess we can get three forks and everyone can pick out what they like." Stowe wrinkles her nose. She's probably grossed out at the idea that her food will be touched by meat. But she's always so hungry, I guess she'll tough it out.

Then Stowe turns to the fresh fruit and vegetable section. "Mmmm. Star fruit, my favorite. Let's get a bag. And what's that odd-looking stuff piled up over there? Looks like a cross between a pineapple and my mother's foot massage ball."

"I believe those fruits are called durian. I've never eaten any, but let's get a couple of the smaller ones, and we can try them later," Ariella suggests.

"We'll need to wash the fruit with sterile water," I say, remembering my mother's worry about diseases. "Remind me when we're ready to eat them. I've brought a laser-sterilizer gun with me."

The cashier hands us the bill. "Wow, I hope this isn't as expensive as it looks. This bill is for 75,000 rupiah!"

"Relax, big spender. It's not that much money. I got 13,900 rupiah for every dollar I exchanged. Here's your 75,000." Stowe hands me a blue 50,000, a green 20,000 and a brown 5,000.

Travel would be easier if everyone used the same money. Anyway, lunch turns out to be less than $6.00 in U. S. dollars.

We share the *nasi campur.* "It's not bad," I say, "even if it's not exactly breakfast food."

"To our stomachs, it's dinner time," Ariella reminds us.

After finishing our "breakfast" we pack the fruit away for later. I jump into the driver's seat but, as usual, Stowe has something to say.

STOWE LEBLOND'S LOG

Borneo, Indonesia

April 11

8:00 AM

We stopped at a market to get some food for our trip. The labels on the food were not in English, obviously, so we had to guess.

The Indonesian diet is based on rice. Many Indonesians are very poor and don't have much to eat besides rice. This can lead to malnutrition. If you can afford it, there are lots of choices. There's gado-gado, which is vegetable salad with peanut sauce. Another vegetarian favorite is tahute-lor, a deep-fried bean curd coated in egg and served with sweet sauce. And for fish lovers, otak-otak, a grilled fish cake wrapped in a banana leaf. I won't bother mentioning the meat and chicken options except to say that you don't see pork anyplace. Most people in Indonesia are Muslim, and they don't eat pork.

Fruits are plentiful so not surprising that a favorite dessert is escampur, a mix of fruits, nuts and jellies served with shaved ice in syrup and coconut.

We do have to be a little careful with what we eat and drink. Water quality can be a problem. Many places do not have water treatment plants, or wells that are tested for bacteria. As a result, people who drink water or eat food washed in tap water can get really sick. Lucky for us, Wheaton has

brought along a couple of hand held lasers that will boil wa-
ter and kill the microbes. So Mom, we are following a few
rules: 1. Don't eat fresh salads. (No gado-gado *for us* ☹ *)*
2. Only eat fruit if we can remove the skin. So no escampur
because of the shaved ice. 3. Make sure we boil our water
before drinking it.

5. HEADING UPRIVER

S towe hops into the passenger seat and gives me a shove. "Maybe you should let Ariella drive. We don't want to attract attention with an 11-year-old behind the wheel."

"I'm perfectly capable of driving the HeliBoaJee. I did invent it, you know." But we *are* on kind of a secret mission, so I move to the back seat.

We head north, and despite our mature driver, people stop and stare. It's not every day you see what looks like a pickup truck cab mounted on top of a speedboat on wheels. And then, of course, there's us. Thanks to my Filipino grandparents, my hair and eyes are dark brown, a lot like the Indonesians, but blonde-haired Stowe, and Ariella with her white braid and pale skin, look nothing like the locals.

Driving out of Ketapang we pass houses painted canary yellow and kelly green. We see kids playing soccer and old men standing by the water fishing. There are nice houses and poor shacks, not a lot of cars, but plenty of motorcycles and bicycles.

We are halfway to Teluk Melano when the skies open up. It's raining so hard we can't see much.

"I hope the road doesn't flood," Ariella says.

"Don't worry. If it does we'll convert to boat form." Nice when I can be the calm one.

As fast as the storm comes, it goes, and in an hour's time we pass the town of Sukadana. It is sitting on a beautiful horseshoe-shaped beach.

"Wish we had time for a swim." You can see the wheels turning in Stowe's head, but she knows we have a long trip in front of us. "Maybe before we leave," she murmurs.

A little further along, we arrive at the town of Teluk Melano sitting at the mouth of the Sungai Melano river.

"Well, guys, this is the end of the road for us. We're going upriver." I feel like we're in one of those movies where you're about to head into the unknown.

We _are_ heading into the unknown.

With the vehicle right at the edge of the water, I take over the controls and convert the HeliBoaJee into its speedboat mode. I call it a speedboat because it's fast. But it's not slim like the fancy speedboats you might see on a lake or bay. The body is an elongated version of the Jeep form of our vehicle, and the sides are a bit higher than your typical motorboat. I guess you could say it's clunky. But, kind of like me, looks aren't everything.

With our vehicle in the water, we slip into life jackets and lather on the sunscreen.

Ariella looks like she belongs out here in her Tilley hat,

long-sleeved khaki shirt and cargo pants. None of her usual black clothes in this climate.

We push off and begin to motor upriver. Before long we leave all civilization behind. The banks of the river are crammed with mangrove trees, their roots pressing into the river bottom. We pass lots of peat swamps. These might come in handy for refueling later.

The air is warm, sort of like New Jersey in August. But it's so humid my sunglasses could use windshield wipers. We're covered in bug spray, but mosquitoes are still close enough to my ears that I can listen to their conversations.

"Good thing you told us to start on our malaria pills before we took off," I say to Ariella as I squash a little bug right before it bites me.

"Yuck," Stowe blurts out. "What is that disgusting smell?"

"Ugh, something does smell gross. Stowe, did you bring stinky socks along and put them inside a bag of onions?"

"I did *not*," she says, as she leans over and pulls out a brown bag with the durian fruit in it. "These must be rotten. Should I throw them overboard?"

"Hold on," Ariella says. "It's probably not spoiled. The heat's brought out the durian's smell. The taste is supposed to be pretty interesting, like onion-flavored custard. Find a plastic bag and store them for now."

Stowe wraps up the fruit. Not sure either one of us is going to be able to eat them later, but we shouldn't throw the fruit in the water. Might wipe out the fish, if they can smell.

Back in the driver's seat I get us going again. An ordinary boat would take six hours to reach the park, but the Heli-BoaJee is no ordinary vessel. It should get us where we're going in a third of the time. It's close to 10:00 AM and I notice that the scenery has changed. "Are those palm trees?"

"I have a feeling we're traveling along a palm oil plantation," Ariella says.

"Palm oil? Is that what makes my hands dirty when I rub them on banisters?" I crack my wise-guy smile.

"No." Ariella laughs, shaking her head. "See those bunches of small, reddish-colored fruits toward the tops of the trees? They may look like plums, but each cluster can weigh 50 pounds, and the oil extracted from them is very valuable. Next time you go to the supermarket check the ingredients on any shelf, and you'll find palm oil listed on lots of products. As you can see, the rainforest has been cut down to make room for the plantation."

"I'm guessing that's not good for the orangutans?" Stowe asks.

"That's right," our grandmother confirms. "Destroy the rainforest, and many species lose their food and shelter."

"And then there are the poachers," I remind everyone.

Stowe's been talking into her headset off and on the whole trip. Wonder if she's paying any attention to her navigating responsibilities. "Nature Girl, any idea where we are?"

There's a short pause while Stowe refocuses. "Oops," she says, pushing the headset microphone away from her mouth. "Guess I wasn't paying attention. Looks like a while ago we needed to hang a right at a tributary heading east."

Before I can answer, we are interrupted by the sound of something crashing through the trees on the bank of the river.

STOWE LEBLOND'S LOG

Borneo, Indonesia

April 11

10:00 AM

We've been traveling up the Sungai Melano river. At the beginning there were other boats, but the farther upriver we go, the more alone we are. There are lots of mangrove trees lining the shores. They grow with their roots in the soil, but the soil is often under the water. Since they need oxygen, they also have roots hanging out higher up, called aerial roots. Mangroves are found on the coastline where the water is salty. Most plants can't handle salt, but the mangroves aren't like most plants. They pump the salt out through their leaves. I'm thinking of doing an experiment when I get home. I'll pour salty water on some of our houseplants to see what happens. Don't worry Mom, I won't kill your prize Schefflera. Anyway, without mangroves and their amazing roots, the riverbanks would erode away.

We got to see a palm oil plantation, although I'm not sure that was a good thing. Palm oil plants are not the same as coconut palms. They are two different species. The palm oil trees are originally from Africa. They grow up to 20 meters (almost the same as 20 yards) tall and they live for around 25 years. These trees are unusual in that they have no branches. If growing conditions are good, they will produce 20-25 leaves/year. Having lots of big leaves is important, since clusters of fruits are produced at the base of each leaf. The fruits have a fleshy, oily outer layer and a single *seed. One tree can produce 10 tons of fruit, which produces 3.9 tons of palm oil.*

Ariella told us that palm oil is big business. The oil is used for lots of things like cooking, makeup and machinery. Indonesia is the largest producer of palm oil in the world, with Borneo and Sumatra the islands where most of these trees grow. For palm oil trees to do well, they need hot temperatures, lots of rain and sun. The tropics are a great place for these plantations. It sure is hot and it rains plenty. But a lot of sun is also required, and that's a problem in a rain forest. So the plantation owners have decided the big trees have to go. The thing about the rainforest is that it's got a lot of biodiversity. That means there are many different kinds of plants, which also means lots of different animals can find places to live and things to eat.

It's not surprising that when you cut down the rainforest and just plant palm oil trees, animals get in trouble. Some pretty cool animals have become endangered, like the Borneo pygmy elephants, crocodiles, sun bears, and orangutans. It would be so cool to see some of those animals on this rescue mission. But since they're endangered, we won't have much chance. Of course, I sure hope we see some orangutans, especially the one we've come to find.

P.S. I wasn't planning to wear make-up, but if it uses palm oil I definitely won't be getting any 😊.

WORDS I'M LEARNING IN INDONESIAN:

Sungai – river

6. A Sun Bear In Trouble

The three of us look up at what appears to be a black bear tearing through the palm oil plantation. In the distance, voices are yelling, and they don't sound friendly.

"Ariella, what's going on?" Stowe whispers.

Ariella's face is as white as her hair. The voices are getting closer. "Exactly what I was worried about. Those may be poachers after that bear. They won't want any witnesses."

"What do we do now?" Stowe's voice gets a little high-pitched. "How long would it take to get us into Heli mode so we can get out of here?"

"Too long," I tell Stowe. "Besides we need to witness this so we can report it. Don't worry, here's what we're going to do. You two duck down in the middle of the boat." I crouch down and enter a command on the HeliBoaJee's computer keyboard. My Wheaton-designed wrapping extends from both sides of the boat, forming a shield around the vehicle. I hope the swishing noise it makes as it extends doesn't attract attention. The wrapping is thin and light like sandwich wrap, but stronger than leather.

"How's this going to protect us?" Stowe whispers. "The covering is see-through."

"It's a light-deflecting skin made of a meta material. Light bends around this material, making us invisible."

Ariella puts her fingers to her lips. Three guys come into the clearing not far from the bear. One of them has a gun.

Our grandmother has the lens of her camera sticking out of a tiny space in the invisible covering. I sure hope those guys don't notice.

We hear a sharp pop, and the bear lets out a horrible wail. Stowe and I are holding hands so tight that we may be stopping each other's blood. After the bear keels over, the poachers wait a couple minutes and then walk over to it.

They're squatting down looking at it from all angles. So weird, they almost look like they care. But then the guys pull the bear onto a stretcher and drag it off into the woods.

Ariella puts her arm around Stowe's trembling shoulder.

We sit there in stunned silence for some time until we're sure the poachers are gone.

"Why would they do that?" Stowe's eyes are loaded with tears.

"That was a Malayan Sun Bear. They're a protected species, so we have just witnessed a crime." Ariella's jaw is tight and her right hand is clenched in a fist.

"Are they going to eat the bear?" Stowe cried.

"They might, but more likely the poachers will sell the body parts for medicine, souvenirs or even decoration. Sun bears are very valuable."

"That's horrible!" Stowe's eyes are wide now, and her angry voice is too loud.

"Shshhh," I say. "The last thing we need is for those guys to realize we're here. I don't want to be another one of their trophies." I give my cousin a nudge.

Ariella puts her hand on top of Stowe's. "It's illegal to kill sun bears, but people don't always follow the law. I've recorded the entire event on my camera. We'll give the pictures to Angga and the other government officials who patrol the forests. Maybe they can find these men and see that they are punished."

"Either way we ought to try finding Angga and the park entrance before the poachers realize we've been watching." My leg is shaking so much it rocks the boat.

When we're sure the hunters are gone, I retract our shield and get it safely stored again. We turn the HeliBoa-Jee around and head back down the river in search of the arm that will lead us to Gunung Palung National Park.

We travel along in silence for a while. Hard to stop thinking about what we've seen.

"Maybe I should've stayed home and hung out with the girls from the ski team," Stowe says. "I don't ever want to see something like that again."

"I know what you mean. I could've finished my robot design project for the Air Force. It's due pretty soon."

"That doesn't sound like fun. No soccer or video games with the guys?"

"What guys?"

"Come on, Wheaton. You must have some friends?"

"Not really. Remember I went to college at a younger age than most kids go to middle school. It's not like the other students were interested in playing with me! They were almost as old as our parents."

"But you must have some friends your own age?"

"Nope. My parents tried to help find me company, but face it, 11-year-old kids do boring stuff I could do when I was three."

"Thanks a lot Wheaton. I'm about your age."

"You're different, Stowe. I wish I could do half the things you do."

Ariella's been peering at the river-bank through her binoculars, but I think she's been listening to us. At one point she turns and gives me a smile. It's an odd thing to say, but my grandmother's been my friend forever.

After a few more minutes of cruising, Ariella puts down her binocs and looks intently at the two of us. "I think you now understand why I want to stay away from poachers. But awful attacks, like we just saw on the sun bear, is one reason biodiversity is at risk. And that is why we started ResQ.

"Looks like we're getting to the end of the palm oil plantation." She points to a place where the landscape changes.

The endless palm oil trees are replaced by a variety of trees in every shape and size. "Funny how after seeing only palm oil trees, all the different species in the rain forest pop out," Stowe remarks.

I always wondered what my mother meant by that saying *you can't see the forest for the trees*. Now I know.

Stowe picks up one of Ariella's cameras and starts photographing the forest. She's so busy taking pictures that we almost miss our turn again. "Less sightseeing and a little more assistance, oh mighty navigator," I say.

Stowe hollers as I make a sharp left into a narrower arm of the river. "Watch out ahead."

We dodge a bunch of floating logs, some individual, some lashed together in rafts. "Wonder where they're coming from?"

We clear these obstacles, and before too much longer arrive at a small wooden dock with a sign – Gunung Palung National Park. "Well, I guess this is it."

STOWE LEBLOND'S LOG

Borneo, Indonesia

April 11

11:00 AM

We just witnessed the poaching of a Malayan sun bear. It was horrible watching that animal get shot. It was so beautiful, even unconscious. Its fur was this shiny jet black, with a light colored crescent-shaped marking on its chest, right under the chin. The sun bear wasn't very big, especially compared with a grizzly or a polar bear. Ariella told us that sun bears range from four to five feet tall, and anywhere from 60-175 pounds. I know plenty of adult humans who are bigger than that. The poor sun bear. It was probably looking for food. Sun bears are omnivores (that means they eat animals and plants). They really like termites, ants, beetle larvae, bee larvae and honey, and a large variety of fruits, especially figs. I get the honey and figs, but have to wonder about the bug diet. Sometimes they even eat the shoots of palm trees. That probably only happens when their nice forest is chopped down so a palm plantation can be built.

7. WELCOME TO GUNUNG PALUNG NATIONAL PARK

"Where is everyone?" Stowe asks.

It does seem deserted. But before we have time to wonder about making another wrong turn, a man comes running up to the dock. He's about Stowe's height, taller than me but short for a grown-up. He has on an olive-green uniform with an emblem of a tree sewn on his shirt, and he's wearing a New York Yankees baseball hat.

"Hello. I thought I heard a boat motor. I am Angga Rezaputra. You must be Ariella Gordon and Stowe LeBlond. And you must be Wheaton Guinto?"

Grrrr. He's looking at all five feet of me, and wondering why I'm so young? "Yup, that's me." I'm not planning to give this guy my biography. My B.S. in Material Science and Engineering is really immaterial to why we're here. Ha. That's pretty funny.

"Welcome. Did you have trouble finding us?" Glad Angga has decided to move on.

As usual, Stowe is the first to speak. "We missed the turn into your part of the river, and ended up motoring along a palm oil plantation. And then we saw some poachers kill a Malayan Sun Bear." Stowe takes a breath, and nudges Ariella, pointing at her camera.

"You have photo? May I look? And how long ago did you witness this bear shooting?"

"About forty-five minutes ago," Ariella tells Angga, handing him her camera.

Angga scrolls through the pictures, zooming in to get a better look at the criminals. Then he lets out a sigh of relief. "Those are not poachers, they are forest rangers."

"And they go around killing endangered species?" Stowe's blue eyes are giving him one of her cold marble stares. "Not sure we should be helping you!"

Angga starts to laugh. "Please listen. We are on same side. What you saw was shooting, but with tranquilizer gun. The bear is fine.

"The problem, these bears have been dislocated. This area is their native home, but palm oil plantations have replaced the bear's forest. So they tear through farms causing lot of damage. Our staff get complaints, so they go in to relocate bear before the plantation owners *do* kill them."

"So when the bear wakes up, it'll be in a new home? Are you sure it'll be okay?" Stowe's eyes are back in their sockets. But now they have water in them. "I know how it feels to be forced to move when you don't want to."

Stowe used to live in Colorado. She told me that when they first moved to Vermont, nothing seemed right.

Angga smiles. "Our ranger relocate bear and then stay a distance away and watch over it. They will not leave until it wakes up and moves normally. I promise this the best way to keep peace between the growers and the wildlife."

"It is a relief to know the sun bear will be okay," Ariella says, putting her arm around Stowe, giving her a little squeeze. "Now we need to focus on what brought us here."

"Yes, indeed. Let us go to park ranger station," Angga says, pointing the way up a path away from the riverbank into the forest.

It's dark and damp, and very warm. Stowe leans over and whispers to me, "You're sniffing like a dog."

"I know. Don't you think it's stinky?"

"You smell decaying logs," Angga says, pointing at the evidence as we proceed down the path. "In rain forests, trees grow fast, and they decay very fast."

It's so moist I can't tell if I'm sweating or the air's full of water. Feels like it could rain at any time. I laugh to myself. That's why they call it a rain forest.

In a short time we arrive at a dark brown wooden structure sitting on stilts. We step into the lower level and climb a ladder that reminds me of the way Stowe and I get into her attic. We walk through a couple of rooms filled with equipment.

Angga points to the threshold. "Go out on porch. I have to check on a few things. I will join you in a minute."

We sit down on a bench at a long table. There's a ceiling fan that helps dry us off, at least a little. The bugs are eyeing us, but from the other side of the screen.

Angga brings us glasses of chrysanthemum tea. I'm guessing this is what water tastes like after you've washed the dishes in it.

While we're "enjoying" our tea, Angga comes back with a large pot. "It is lunch time here at the research station." He gives each of us a small bowl with rice and ladles something into each.

"*Soto?*" Ariella says with a smile. Angga nods.

"Thank you," says Ariella. "Kids, this is an Indonesian specialty. It's delicious."

Looks like chicken with rice soup to me. I glance over at Stowe. She's eating the soup, being careful to dodge the chicken. Best way to keep Angga from noticing her food problem is to change the subject. And right on cue Stowe switches gears.

"Any news on the baby orangutan?"

8.   WHAT ABOUT THE BABY ORANGUTAN?

Angga's at the head of the table now. "Everyone keep an eye out for the missing baby orangutan, but so far no sightings."

Where are all these other people he keeps referring to? No one's here but Angga.

"One week ago I arrive at park headquarters for my shift. Some scientists out in the park found Bella in great distress. They thought she was wailing because she was shot in the palm of her right hand."

"So she couldn't swing through the trees?"

"That's right, Stowe." Angga continues. "But we keep track of the adult orangutans in our forest. So we figure out that Bella has bigger problems than being shot. She has one-year-old baby, and he is missing."

"But don't most animals leave their mothers by the time they're a year old?"

"For most animals that is correct. But orangutans only have one offspring at a time. The juvenile stay with its mother, learning how to survive, for 6 to 8 years before heading out alone."

"So where is Bella now? Is she still out there?" Stowe asks.

"No." Angga points his chin in the direction of an out-building next to the ranger station. "We brought Bella here to treat her wound. Also to keep her safe from predators. With her hand damaged she limps on ground on three of her four limbs."

"And there are predators that could kill her?" Stowe's shoulders hunch up.

"Yes," Angga nods. "In a few minutes we will go out and say hello to Bella."

Stowe presses on. "Who do you think shot her?"

"Yeah. Who shoots a mother in front of its baby?" I can't believe anyone could do something like that.

"We are not sure," Angga tells us. "The best explanation, poachers shot Bella so they could grab Buddi, our name for her baby. Hard to know if he still nearby or even in Borneo, but we have to make effort to find him. These babies very important to the future of this species.

"I contacted ResQ because the park pretty big and, as you can see, I do not have much help."

I lean close to Stowe. "I'll say. Looks like Angga's the only one here."

Me and my big mouth. Of course, Angga hears me. "The park is 900 square kilometers, and we have a lot to do. We monitor and protect the wildlife—plants and animals—run programs for tourists, *and* guard against poachers. Most days staff is scattered throughout the park. And as I told you on phone, some of my people have gone for training.

"From what I read about ResQ, you specialize in finding animals. Your website say you have some unique equipment?"

"Yup, we do!" I look at Ariella and Stowe's expectant eyes. The device I've brought is so new, even Ariella hasn't seen it yet.

"You know how dogs are trained to sniff objects from missing people, and then their noses save the day?"

I go over to one of our packs and pull out a round box about the size of a cookie tin, except it's titanium. "Allow me to introduce the Finder, my latest invention."

I slide open the top. "Please don't breathe on it or touch the inside."

"It looks like a piece of carpet someone had left over in the basement," Stowe says.

She is so helpful.

"The magic is what you can't see," I explain. "You're looking down at bundles of tiny tubes—carbon nanotubes—billions of them. If you could see them, they would look like a sea of soda straws standing up on end—"

"And these straws, I mean carbon nanotubes, will help us find the baby orangutan, how?"

Stowe needs to give me a chance to finish describing things.

"We need to use the scent of Buddi from somewhere, and suck off molecules from the air space around the object. The chemicals that make up his smell will stick to the inside of the tubes.

"In the field we will release the Finder, which will fly just above the ground. It will pull air from whatever is at the surface. If chemicals in the air match what's in any of the tubes, a signal will be beamed to us saying Buddi was here."

"Sounds like a bionic dog." Stowe makes a sniffing noise.

"You get the idea. Cross between a dog and a drone."

Angga has been staring at the Finder, just listening until now. "You came here in boat. How will you trail this flying dog of yours?"

"Good question," I say, winking at Stowe and Ariella. "We call our vehicle a HeliBoaJee, because it converts from Boat to Jeep to Helicopter. We'll be flying when we launch the Finder."

"Your inventions are impressive. We certainly do not have anything like them," says Angga.

"Thanks." I never know what to say when I get a compliment, so best to move us along. "We need to suck the air from something that Buddi touched, through the Finder. Any suggestions?"

"Your best bet, pull a scent from Bella. Can you do it without hurting her?"

"She has so much hair, maybe we can run a comb over her back and use the hair that comes off?" Funny that Stowe suggests anything having to do with a comb, given what her scrambled-egg head looks like most of the time. But it's a good idea.

Angga gets up. "Sounds like time to visit Bella."

STOWE LEBLOND'S LOG

Borneo, Indonesia

April 11

noon

If I wondered how it was possible for Wheaton to have graduated from college and already be accepted to graduate school, I get it now. He really is a genius! He's invented this thing he calls the Finder. It doesn't look like much—a cross between a cookie tin and a flying saucer. But, as Wheaton said, it's what you can't see.

First, there are the carbon nanotubes. Carbon hexagonal rings all get linked together into sheets. The sheets get rolled into tiny tubes, which stand up on end at the base of the Finder. No idea how Wheaton does this, because you can't see any of this stuff with your naked eyes. He uses special equipment at Stevens Institute, his old University in Hoboken, New Jersey.

Figure the carbon nanotubes are really thin. There are something like five million in an inch. You get the picture. The Finder has hundreds of millions, maybe billions of these things.

Second thing you can't see, are the chemicals that create smells. You know how Dad smells when he comes home after eating a sub with onions? Or how the gym smells at the end of the day? Well, everyone has smells. Not just because they don't take a bath or eat something stinky. The odors come from chemicals we give off on our breath and through our skin. Wheaton says these chemicals are "volatile," meaning they float around in the air after they leave our bodies. The chemicals are just like a fingerprint, our unique smelly signature. So they're different for every person. That's how dogs, with their supersensitive noses, can sniff the clothes of someone who's missing, and then help police find the person.

The Finder imitates the dog nose in being able to detect those chemical signatures. Its "nose" is made of the carbon nanotubes. If chemicals from the missing people, even tiny amounts, are hanging around in the air, chances are, one of the nose nanotubes will "sniff" them. Wonder what an electronic bark sounds like? ☺

It would be cool if the Finder helps find Buddi.

9. BELLA

I grab the Finder and the three of us follow Angga out of the building and across the way to an outdoor enclosed pen.

There, sitting in a hammock, is the saddest looking orange mop of an animal I've ever seen. She's stretched half way across her bed, maybe three and a half feet, and kind of squat.

"We had veterinarian come up from the International Animal Rescue (IAR) organization in Sungai Awan where some orphaned orangutans live."

"Where is that?" Stowe inquires.

"About 30 minutes outside of Ketapang, where you landed," Angga says.

Stowe looks at me, lifting her eyebrows. "We've got to visit," she whispers.

"The vet took out bullet from Bella's hand and gave her some antibiotics. We change her bandage every few days but she is not so happy for our advances—"

"You can't blame her," Stowe blurts out.

"True," Angga says, nodding. "First we feed her pills, some, what are they called, tranquilizers? While she is resting, we examine her and redress the wound.

"We keep her here for a while, hoping Buddi would appear. But we cannot care for her much longer. She need to go to IAR."

"When Bella's healed, they'll set her free, right?" Stowe is not a fan of any form of animal captivity.

"Oh yes, Bella will be released back into the wild. Of course, we hope that before that happens, you find Buddi and they get back together."

"Speaking of which," I say, to keep us on track, "any ideas for how we can get some hair off of Bella?"

"Do you think you can get enough smell of Buddi from the hammock?" Angga asks, noting that the orangutan has been rolling around in a bunch of leaves she matted up on it.

"That should work. All we need are a few molecules from Buddi."

Stowe frowns at me. "Buddi and Bella always travel together. How will we be able to tell Buddi's smell from his mama's?"

"You're right, that is an issue." I turn to Angga. "This may sound silly, but has Bella had a bath lately? We are going to need to be able to separate Bella's chemical signature from Buddi's."

"No bath." Angga smiles at me. "But before bullet was removed from her arm, the vet washed it."

"Which means, we should be able to get a scent that's just Bella's." I nod to Stowe who chimes in.

"And then you can compare that signal with the one from the rest of her, and figure out which belongs to Buddi?"

"Bingo. I haven't tried this before, but it should work."

Now for the first challenge. I turn to Angga. "How are we going to get Bella off her hammock?" No way I'm wrestling that orangutan for access to her bed.

Angga smiles. "We invite her with some treats." He walks over to a bin right outside Bella's pen and pulls out a bunch of fruits.

Stowe sniffs, and wrinkles her nose. "Hmm, the sweet smell of ripe onion custard again. Would that be durian you've got there?"

"Yes. You know durian?" Angga cracks a smile. "Favorite of the orangutan."

"Can't miss the smell, that's for sure." Stowe giggles.

Angga places the cut up durian in the far corner of the pen. Bella seems to perk up, and with a little difficulty hops off the hammock and limps over to her version of an ice cream sundae. While she's feasting, Angga opens the pen and I walk over to the hammock. He stands between me and eyeshot of Bella.

I've got to be quick. With the hose over the hammock, I turn on the vacuum. Bella startles at the sound and stares in my direction.

"Is she coming?" I ask, my leg starting to shake.

"No. Not leaving her durian, and the tranquilizer we use an hour ago has not worn off. But do not take too long."

No need to worry about that. I'm sure my mother wishes I'd vacuum my room as fast as I'm sucking at the airspace above this hammock.

"Okay, that's done. Now for the hard part. Getting an air sample off of Bella's clean, injured arm." I look at Angga, hoping he can help me out here.

"Can you make that hose reach out more?" he asks, gesturing at the air sampler.

"Not really. Do you guys have any pipes, or any kind of narrow tubing?"

Angga pauses. "Yes, I think we have some left over plastic piping. It is pretty thin. We used for plumbing repair. Will that work?

"Maybe. Could you get it for me, please. And hurry," I say, keeping an eye on Bella at all times.

Angga goes and brings back a piece of tubing around 6 feet long. I rig it up to the vacuum end of the scent collector. "Now for the hard part, pulling in our sample without freaking Bella out."

I turn on the instrument so the vacuum suction is gentle, like you'd use on a shaggy carpet. I move the wand in the orangutan's direction. She startles again, but then becomes curious. As the vacuum approaches her arm, she swats at it.

Hope that's all she swats at. My knees are signaling their own distress.

"She's playing with you, Wheaton," Ariella whispers. "Take your time and I bet she'll let you run the wand close to her arm."

Sure enough, I'm able to get the vacuum close enough that the hair on her arm stands straight up. Now I just hope I've captured two distinct chemical signatures.

"Done." I'm getting out of this pen before Bella decides this isn't fun anymore.

Stowe helps me pack away the Finder, and we head back to the ranger station conference porch.

"Angga, where do you suggest we start the search?" Ariella asks.

"My staff found Bella about halfway between here and Sukadana."

"That cool beach we passed?"

Good old Stowe, still thinking about going for a swim.

Angga nods. "My kids love swimming there."

"So if Buddi was captured it would have been in that area?" Not waiting for an answer, I take charge.

"We need to launch the HeliBoaJee in helicopter mode and deploy the Finder. Then we'll direct it to criss-cross the park between here and Sukadana. If Buddi is still in the area we should pick up his scent. Sound like a plan?"

Not waiting for an answer I continue. "It's possible that the poachers could be operating from the coast, not the interior. Or we could go in the wrong direction. Would it be more efficient if we split up in two teams?"

The forest ranger weighs in. "I plan to take Bella to Sukadana by boat, where staff from rescue station meet me to take her. It makes sense for me to cruise perimeter of park and search for baby. But I need someone with me if I spot Buddi. I cannot manage boat, Bella and capture of Buddi by myself."

Stowe and I look at each other, and then turn to look at Ariella. No way do the two of us want to be separated.

"Don't even think you kids are going off without me." Our grandmother gives us a penetrating stare.

"We really can handle this," I plead. "Besides, we're not going to swoop down into the poachers' camp and grab Buddi. We're just going to see if we can scope out where he is. And we'll talk by satellite phone every thirty minutes or so."

"I'm not comfortable—" Ariella hasn't finished her thought when the door to the ranger station flings open.

A big smile comes across Angga's face. "I think solution has arrived."

STOWE LEBLOND'S LOG

Borneo, Indonesia

April 11

1:00 PM

We're here to rescue a young orangutan that got separated from its mother. This is a bad thing, since these little
guys are dependent upon their mothers until they are six or
seven years old. They nurse until they're six! Sounds a little
gross to me.

Orangutan means person of the forest, because that's
where they live. They're only found in two places, Sumatra and Borneo, both islands in Indonesia. (Same locations
where most of the palm oil plantations are!!) Their ape cousins, the gorillas, chimpanzees and bonobos all live in Africa.
Of course, Wheaton and I are a different kind of cousins, but
glad we live on the same continent 😊.

Orangutans usually live alone, not like gorillas that live
in troops. Pairs of female orangutans and their babies meet
up for what scientists call feeding aggregations – their version of a Friday night pizza party. You can tell males from
females if you know a few things about them, aside from
the obvious. Males develop cheek pads they use to throw the
sound of their long calls. They're twice as big as the females,
which makes sense. But males tend to have longer hair. Go
figure.

Orangutans have well developed hands. In fact, their
extremities look more like four hands than two hands and

two feet. The thumbs and toes are what's called opposable – meaning the thumb and big toe can touch the other digits independently. Very handy – ha, ha. They do great traveling from branch to branch and on the ground. But safer to be up in the trees!

They build nests in trees, and Angga told me they build a new one every night! I can't imagine moving every day. I hated moving and only did it once in my whole life. (I'm fine now, Mom, so don't worry.) And this is funny—sometimes they even build a simple nest during the day in case they want to take a rest.

Their favorite food is fruit, and one of the reasons the young stay with their mothers so long is so they can teach their offspring which foods are okay to eat, where to find them and in what seasons. They eat up to 300 different kinds of fruit. It was pretty easy to learn to identify blueberries and raspberries on our walks at home. But I sure wouldn't have wanted to learn 300 fruits, especially if a mistake could make me sick. Or worse! There are many times when fruits are scarce in the tropical rain forest. Then the orangutans have to rely on fallback foods like leaves, the inner bark of trees, ants, termites and flowers. So they have a lot to learn before venturing out alone.

Angga told us that orangutans travel around 1 kilometer per day

MATH PROBLEMS – CONVERTING THE METRIC SYSTEM INTO OUR ENGLISH SYSTEM

1 kilometer = 0.62 miles

10. RAFI

A teenaged boy enters, his heavy backpack catching on the side of the entry way as he stomps onto the porch. He's about Angga's height, but even thinner. He's not in a park uniform, just khaki cargo pants and a t-shirt with a picture of a rock band whose name, Saptarasa, is printed at the bottom.

"*Halo Ayah*," he says to Angga.

"*Halo Anak*. Meet our guests—Ms. Ariella Gordon, her granddaughter Stowe, and her grandson Wheaton. And please speak English, they are from America." Angga turns to us. "This is Rafi. It is school vacation and he is helping me."

"I think *anak* means son," I whisper to Stowe.

"Very good, Wheaton. You understand Indonesian?"

"Nah. My other grandmother and grandfather are Filipino, and they speak Tagalog with my Dad. *Anak* means son in their language so I was guessing."

"Hello," Rafi says, shaking Ariella's hand and then laying his fingers on his chest. He turns to me for a high-five. "Hi, man." Rafi looks at Stowe and waits until she puts her hand out. He gives it a very light shake. Stowe puts her hand to her heart.

Her face doesn't look that red after she's been cross-country skiing. What's all that about?

"Rafi, come sit down for a few minutes. These people come over to help rescue Buddi. They have amazing search tools. We have been discussing splitting into two teams to increase chance we find the baby ape."

"If the poachers did not sell already. Or some predator eaten it." Bingo. Rafi pressed Stowe's button.

"Like what kind of predator?" Stowe interrupts.

"Humans are number one," says Rafi, lifting one finger for emphasis. "But there are others like Sunda Clouded Leopard."

"We've seen them at the Smithsonian Conservation Biology Institute." Stowe looks at Ariella. "They're beautiful, but pretty aggressive, aren't they?"

"They are rare and nocturnal. You be lucky to see one." Rafi smirks at us.

"And you will *not* be out there at night," Ariella says, speaking much louder than usual.

Angga taps his knuckles on the table to get us back on track.

"Rafi, you go with Wheaton and Stowe. They have special convertible-vehicle, helicopter, jeep or boat, so you can search interior."

"Sorry Angga, but I'm still uncomfortable with the kids going off on their own," Ariella says, wrapping her braid around her hand.

"I understand. But GPS out here is not always reliable. We lost Buddi. I don't want to lose three of you. Rafi has spent his entire fifteen years in this park. He knows every square kilometer. The kids in good hands with him."

"And I do need help with Bella, and Buddi, if we find him first."

Ariella purses her lips and nods. "You kids need to check in with us every few hours." Then she gives us one of her *I'm serious* looks.

"Good, then it's settled. Ariella and I take Bella in my boat. We look for Buddi along river at the park perimeter. Whether we find young offspring or not, we need to get Bella to IAR for care. We stay in close contact, and if either team locate Buddi we call each other right away. Yes?"

"Yes, *Ayah*." Rafi says.

"We promise. But don't worry, we'll be fine." Stowe is talking to Ariella but she is looking at Rafi.

Never mind that I'm the one that will get us from here to there.

The five of us walk back down to the river to pick up our vehicles.

"Do you have sufficient fuel in the HeliBoaJee?" Ariella still seems concerned about us separating.

"Sure, but don't worry. If we run low, we'll touch down in a peat swamp and I'll refuel with my methane concentrator."

"Remember, peat swamp sink under heavy weight so don't put that Heli... thing of yours down on the bog," Angga warns.

"Oh, we know," Stowe says, a little too quickly.

Ariella looks puzzled by Stowe's comment.

"Let's get your gear for you," I say, changing the subject. I leap onto the HeliBoaJee and hand Ariella her duffel bag.

She pulls out one of her cameras and hands it to Stowe. "See what you can capture."

Whenever they're together, Ariella gives Stowe some photography instruction. Letting her take one of our grandmother's expensive cameras is a real vote of confidence.

"Oh, wow, thanks. I'll get some great images for you." Stowe's blushing again, and she's not even looking at Rafi.

Before Angga and Ariella get into his boat, he hands Stowe a map of the park. "This is topographic map with some landscape features to help keep you on course. Rafi know the way, but you should have idea where things are too."

Without roads to guide us, I sure hope we don't lose our way. *Again.*

Of course, now we have Rafi. Aren't we lucky?

STOWE LEBLOND'S LOG

Borneo, Indonesia

April 11

1:30 PM

We're off to the interior of the Gunung Palung National Park. This park is the smallest of 8 National Parks in Kalimantan (the Indonesian part of Borneo). It's 900 square kilometers in size. That's about the size of Rocky Mountain National Park, which is around 400 square miles. That's big. We never saw the whole park when we lived in Colorado.

TIME FOR A MATH PROBLEM: 1 square kilometer = 0.386 square miles

900 square kilometer X 0.386 = 347.4 square miles

Gunung Palung became a National Park in 1990. It's the only national park on the west side of the country. It has mangroves, fresh water and peat swamps, forests, mountains, and lots of wildlife including around 2,500 orangutans. In 2018 scientists used drones and flew over Borneo counting nests. From those counts they figured out that there are 70,000-100,000 orangutans left on the island. That may seem like a lot, but in the last 60 years the numbers have dropped from 230,000. That makes each animal super precious, which is why we have to find little Buddi, the lost baby.

Some of the Gunung Palung rainforest is called a primary rainforest. That means it has never been logged or burned down. Primary forests contain the trees that have always been there. The problem is that people are logging and burning primary rainforest so they can plant palm oil plantations or start farms. If later on forests grow up in these areas again, they are considered secondary forests. You can tell the difference by the size of the trees. Primary tropical rain forests may have trees so big that four people holding hands can't reach around the trunk. In secondary forests there will be trees with small trunk sizes or logs lying on the ground.

WORDS I'M LEARNING IN INDONESIAN:

Halo – Hello

Ayah – Father

Anak – Son (Wheaton told us it's the same word in Tagalog)

11. Bogged Down Again

The three of us walk up to the HeliBoaJee .

"This is different." Rafi paces the length of our vehicle scratching his head. "It is going to fly?"

"You bet it is. Hop in and sit in the middle while I begin the transformation," I say to Rafi and Stowe.

Prepare to be amazed, oh child of the rainforest.

With them seated, I enter a command into the HeliBoaJee computer to extend the sides and shoot the top over our craft. Another command sends out the tail. "Hold onto your seats, the HeliBoaJee's now going to change shape." As I type in directions, the boat's ends pull in, and the sides widen. Next, I extend the rotor. As it begins to whir, we lift out of the water. Then, with two hands, I pull down on the levers, lowering the landing skids, we will need later.

"Awesome. Who makes these HeliBoaJee things?"

"It's one of a kind. Wheaton designed and built it. He can make anything." Stowe sounds proud of me. "You should see all his inventions."

Enough about me. "Let's get going."

We wave goodbye to Ariella and Angga and lift off. As we move up over the dense forest canopy, the ground below us disappears.

Stowe's busy getting her blonde cheese doodle hair into a ponytail and pulling on her blue Ski Vermont baseball hat.

"You ski?" Rafi asks Stowe.

"Yea, pretty much all I do at home. It's great, but it's nice to be doing something so different for a change."

"She's a champion. When she's older she may be in the Olympics," I tell Rafi. My cousin's an amazing skier, but she doesn't show off.

"Wheaton exaggerates."

"I don't, but never mind. Stowe, could you please take the Finder out of its case," I request.

"What is that thing?" Rafi asks.

"It's a cross between a bionic dog and a drone."

"Cool, a drone." Rafi flies his hand over our heads and grins. "But what is a bionic dog?"

"It's not really a dog. It's material I've designed to detect chemicals produced by people or animals. I'll explain this better when we have more time. But you'll get the idea when it sniffs out Buddi.

"For now, Stowe will control the Finder's movements, but you need to chart the course it will take and serve as our navigator." He might as well make himself useful if he has to come with us.

Rafi sits next to me in front of the computer screen and instrument panel. I show him how to slide the system back and forth as needed by different operators. Then I explain the navigation system.

"Got it." Rafi gives me a strong nod. He reviews the options and turns to me. "Follow stream below. Use it as our guide, and travel west in zig-zag pattern."

"On our way," I confirm. "Please slide the system over to Stowe so she can deploy the Finder."

Under my direction, she releases my latest, and hopefully, greatest invention. "Now go ahead and bring up the Finder app, to follow its movements on the screen."

With everyone focused on their jobs, we get to work.

Following Rafi's suggestion, I fly the HeliBoaJee to the left and right of the stream. But the forest is so dense that half the time the stream disappears under the treetops, like a garter snake beneath a bush.

Stowe's working hard to keep the Finder on course. Her eyes are glued to the screen as she controls its movements. "I can't see where the Finder is, except on the screen," she says, peering out the window at the tree-tops. "But we're getting a signal. Maybe Buddi's down there."

"Only one way to tell. Rafi, help me find a break in the canopy so we can get on the ground and look around. Stowe, direct the Finder to the same location and sit it down. We can activate it again after we land."

We continue to zig and zag for a while. "There," Rafi points, "your way in to forest floor."

I see a small opening from the sky to the ground. "Hold on," I yell, as I guide the HeliBoaJee through a little window into the forest.

The ground is coming up fast, so I get us into position just in time for our landing skids to touch down, or rather slump to a standstill.

When the rotor blade stops twirling I stand up and immediately notice a wobble. "Hmm, weird. What's that about?"

Stowe leaps out in her usual not-looking-first style. "Rocket Scientist, did you forget Angga's warning about landing on a bog? Remember what happened to me in the Pine Barrens?"

"Yikes." I look out the window at the landing skid. The bog has sucked in around it. I wonder about its depth. "At least the other skid's on firm ground."

"Rafi, can you ease out of here without rocking this thing more? Then, you and Stowe grab hold of the HeliBoaJee and hang on. I'll stay on board and move to the same side, and maybe with all our weight, we can tilt the ship out of the bog."

Of course, the three of us don't weigh nearly enough to produce the desired effect. For a moment their feet go airborne, and it seems we're going to topple. But then the craft lodges in position.

I grab some rope, secure it to the HeliBoaJee and throw the other end to Rafi who ties it to a nearby tree. Now that we have insured it won't tip further, I join the others on the ground.

Stowe and Rafi have launched the Finder again and are heading after it. I wish they'd let me figure out how much trouble the HeliBoaJee is in first.

"We can't afford to get lost out here," I call out. "I'll mark the trees with red X's as we go." Not sure they're listening. I hurry to catch up, trying not to trip over all the roots sticking out of the soil.

Stowe's pointing ahead. "The Finder's heading up the side of that tree."

The three of us reach the base of a big trunk. We tilt our heads all the way back, staring into the green horizon. It looks as dense from the forest floor as from the air.

I shake my head. "I know my Finder's better than that. Why is it so confused? I can't see any baby in that tree."

"They are pretty hard to see from the ground. I have harness to climb trees," Rafi says. "I go check it out."

Before we can object, Rafi hoists himself up the tree. In no time he propels back down to where we're waiting. "No baby," he tells us. "But I did see a nest."

I grab my binoculars and peer up. "What does a nest have to do with a baby orangutan? It's not a bird." I thought this dude knew his way around the place.

"Wheaton, that's where orangutans sleep," Stowe says to me while looking at Rafi. I'm sure he gets that she knows all this stuff and I don't.

"And since there's no baby, there's still the problem of knowing whether the Finder has picked up Buddi or Bella's scent, right?" Stowe asks.

Using the Finder app on my cell phone, I program in the scent from Bella's clean leg, on the Finder's channel one. I assign channel two for the chemical signature I got off the hammock, which should contain both Buddi and his mother's odors. Then we send our bionic dog back up the tree.

The Finder sniffs through one channel and then the other. The three of us crowd around my phone watching as one, and then two tracings appear. Both channels pick up signals from the nest, and they match perfectly.

"They were together," I show them.

"And we know Bella was shot a distance from here," Rafi comments. "Maybe, nest was used before Buddi separated from his mother."

"Like how long before?" I ask.

Rafi shrugs. "Orangutans build new nests almost every night, so if the *bayi* is one year old or more, he and his *ibu* could have used nest months ago."

"That's a pretty complex nest." I may not know much about the natural world, but I do know something about engineering. "They build a new one every night? That's crazy."

"And you are looking at an abandoned home." Rafi tell us. "These are great architects. First orangutans build the base, strong enough to hold them. Then they take green leafy branches and make themselves a mattress, and sometimes they even make pillows and a canopy to keep dry."

"And looks like they've created some sort of fastener to the tree." These orangutans must be the engineers of the rainforest.

"So why move every night?"

"Not sure, Stowe. I guess they need to move around to find food, and too much trouble to always return home," Rafi says.

"Guys, this natural history lesson is going to need to wait. If we plan to find Buddi, we need to get the HeliBoaJee back in the air. Remember, one skid is stuck in the bog."

"Your fault, Aero-King."

"Well, if you hadn't jumped out the way you did, Snow Queen, the skid might not have gotten wedged in."

"Quiet a second," Rafi puts his fingers to his lips. "Do you hear that?"

We nod as we listen to high-pitched whirring and grinding.

"My dad's chainsaw sounds like that when he's cutting wood. Let's follow the noise. Maybe we can find some help." Stowe turns to run in the direction of the sound.

"Wait," Rafi sticks out his arm to break Stowe's movement.

Stowe wrinkles her forehead and pushes Rafi's arm away. But before she can give him some of her classic lip, the cell phone rings. Stowe picks up. "Hi, Ariella. Have you found Buddi? Where are you guys?"

Stowe turns to me. "She says no luck yet. They're on the southern edge of the park. And she's annoyed with us. She expected a call by now."

Stowe goes on to tell Ariella about the nest we found, and then informs her of our mishap. "I know Angga warned us. Sorry. But there seem to be some people not too far away. We're on our way to ask for some help."

Stowe mouths to me that Angga's been listening too, and wants to talk to Rafi.

He takes the phone and pulls it a little away from his ear as Angga starts to yell. The conversation is all in Indonesian. We don't know what's being said, but the angry tone is the same in every language. After a few minutes, we hear Rafi say, "*Sampaijumpalagi,*" as he hangs up. "We could be in big trouble," he mutters, as he stuffs his satellite phone deep in his backpack.

12. LOSING RAFI

"That chain saw noise you heard before," Rafi says in a whisper, "probably comes from loggers. They might have heard us."

"That's good right? They can help dislodge the HeliBoa-Jee?" Stowe's voice is too loud for Rafi's liking, and he slaps his hand over her mouth.

She looks at me in panic, but before I can say something, Rafi hisses at us. "No questions now. We go to that belian tree over there. I think the trunk is wide enough to hide us."

No clue what's going on, but Rafi's made it clear this is not the time for a debate. We make a mad dash and crouch down, following our fearless leader's instructions. We continue to hear shouting in the distance. Hard to tell if it's getting closer or not.

"What's going on?" Not sure I want to know.

"The noise we're hearing probably from illegal loggers. Sorry if I smacked you, Stowe, but trust me, those guys are not interested in helping us. And they do not like being observed."

"Don't worry about it. Are the loggers as bad as poachers?" Stowe looks kind of pale, and not because she's wearing sunscreen.

Rafi raises his eyebrows. "They have chainsaws."

There goes my leg doing its shaking dance. This is way more adventure than I need. "I hope those guys don't see the marks I put on the trees to help us find our way back, or even worse, discover the HeliBoaJee."

Stowe is holding my hand tight. A lake seems to be forming between our palms, and I don't think it's the high humidity.

As we wait, I glance up and see a green snake draped around the branch right next to me. I nudge Stowe, turning my head and eyes in the direction of the tree.

"Be quiet and hold still," she mouths, without letting out a sound. I get the message.

A few minutes pass, and the voices of the loggers seem to be getting farther away. Not true for the snake.

"I'm pretty sure that's a pit viper," Stowe whispers. "Aren't they venomous?"

Rafi nods. But he doesn't seem worried. "They are nocturnal. So try not to scare it. Stay low and start moving away from the tree. No quick move."

Snakes are not my thing. I hold onto Stowe's hand, and try to make my feet follow hers. That is, until my foot slips and sends a loose twig flying.

As the twig hits the tree, the viper's triangular head lunges forward toward the incoming sound. We watch, frozen in place, until the nighttime creature coils back to its resting spot in the crook of the tree.

Once a safe distance away, we stand up. Of course, Stowe can't resist pulling out the camera to snap some photos to show Ariella. Not sure our grandmother will be thrilled to know we were so close to a viper.

"Nature Girl, whenever you finish, can we go back to the HeliBoaJee? I need to figure out a way to get it dislodged from the bog."

A few drops of rain hit my nose. "I hope the marks on the trees don't wash off."

"No worries. I know the way," Rafi says, grinning at me.

Whatever. It isn't raining hard, and we can see enough of my red X's leading back to the HeliBoaJee. We don't need to rely on Rafi's rainforest brilliance.

The HeliBoaJee hasn't straightened out in our absence.

"Before we leave this spot, I'm thinking maybe this would be a good place to refuel. We can use our concentrator to suck some methane out of this bog."

"Wig, you are unreal sometimes. Since we failed to attract the chainsaw guys the first time, let's see if we can make enough noise to be sure they find us!"

"I see your point. Let's get out of here and we'll touch down somewhere else to refuel."

I look around for something we can use to pry that skid out of the bog. "Look over there." I point to a few large tree limbs lying on the ground. "Those look like perfect levers. Let's get them under the skid."

"Great idea, Hercules. And how do you think the three of us will move those limbs? Have you been power lifting in your spare time?"

"Okay, so that wasn't such a good idea. How about this? I do have a winch on board. Maybe we can wrap a chain around that big tree over there," I point. Then I can use it to pull us out of the bog?"

"Sound better," Rafi says. "Stowe, take my backpack and get on board. Wheaton, give me the end of the chain. I will climb the tree and get it se-cured. Once you straighten us out, I will join you and we get out of here."

Just like before, Rafi demon-strates his climbing skills and secures the chain around the tree. I start reeling the He-liBoaJee out of the bog. Of course, that gener-ates some noise.

"Uh-oh." Rafi calls out from his perch. "I see company coming. Take off *now*. I text you to pick me up later."

Stowe and I look at each other. I don't think either one of us thinks this sounds like such a great plan.

"Get out of here," Rafi shouts. His tone doesn't leave any room for further discussion, so I power up.

As the HeliBoaJee lifts, we see two men in camouflage pants and black t-shirts running and pointing in our direction. They're not tall, but you could imagine them doing well in a wrestling match. They have heavy rope draped across their chests. I'd like to think they only use it to tie up the logs they harvest.

"That must be the chainsaw gang," I mutter.

It's hard to see the ground now. Stowe takes out her binoculars, sweeping them across the ground below us in every direction. "Rafi," she hollers, but he has vanished.

13. SEARCHING FOR RAFI

"What are we going to do now? Rafi's supposed to help us navigate. Do you have a clue where we are? We can't abandon him out here." Stowe's still staring through the binoculars, as she lists all the problems associated with losing Rafi.

I have to admit I didn't see the point to Rafi coming with us. My leg, on the other hand, is reminding me of how important he is to our survival.

And when we think things can't get any worse, a phone starts ringing from Rafi's backpack. The one he's going to use to call us later...

Neither of us wants to, but we better pick up. I'm busy flying the HeliBoaJee so I ask Stowe to dig out the phone and see who's calling.

"Hi, this is Stowe. Rafi's gone off to do something, and asked me to pick up."

"Angga's on the other end and he wants to know what's going on," she mouths.

Then she returns to her conversation with Rafi's father. "Things are fine....Yes, we stayed away from the loggers, no problem....Rafi's gone to find a good refueling spot and then we'll continue searching.... I'll have Rafi call you as soon as he gets back. Bye."

She hangs up before having to continue stretching the truth. But at this point the actual facts won't help. And Rafi was supposed to watch out for us. If Angga finds out we got separated, there will be big trouble. I sure hope he couldn't hear the Heli blades in the background.

Stowe's chewing on her lip, a sure sign that she feels guilty about the story she just told. But as my mother says, guilt is a useless emotion, so I guess we should focus on finding Rafi. Not saying my mother thinks lying's a good thing.

"What are we going to do now?" Stowe asks. "Should we go back and search on the ground?"

"Not unless you want to come face to face with the chainsaw gang. Here's a better option." Time to bring out my **Binoculaser**.

"Put this on." I hand Stowe a helmet. "Pull down on the binoculars. The ocular cups will suck around your eyes."

"And what do I do with these that's so special?" Stowe asks, her head bobbing under the weight of my latest invention.

"Point your face toward the ground outside," I direct her. "You can see through these lenses, same as a normal set of binoculars. But now put your finger on the side of your helmet. Can you feel a couple of buttons?"

"Yup."

"The top button on the right side of your helmet will deploy a very narrow, high-powered scope attached to a miniature camera. As you shoot photos with the button below it, they will come up on our computer screen, kind of like a movie. When leaves get in the way, push the button on the left side of your helmet. A low energy laser pulse will be emitted from the camera, creating a small hole through the canopy. Then you can continue photographing."

"Should we be worrying about your laser hurting someone or something?"

"Fair question. These are special lasers designed to burn through cellulose, the major component of cell walls. If they come upon an object without a cell wall they'll bend around it. Only plants and fungi have cell walls."

"Okayyy. Let's see how this works finding Rafi." Stowe doesn't sound convinced. But she will be.

I decide to quit hovering and fly in a spiral out from where we lifted off. "How's the Binoculaser working for you?"

Stowe gives me a thumbs up. She's busy peering down from the open side of the HeliBoaJee. "What do the images look like on the screen?" Stowe asks. She keeps trying to turn and look, but when she takes her eyes away from the ground, she has to stop photographing.

"Nothing yet, just a lot of rain forest."

It doesn't take long for Stowe to get frustrated. "Where could Rafi have gone?"

"I don't know. Hope those chainsaw guys didn't capture him."

Stowe flips up the Binoculaser. "Should we go and find their logging site?"

"I was thinking the same thing. But we need to be careful and stay above the canopy so those dudes can't see us."

"Even if they can't see us, won't they hear us?"

Funny, Stowe thinking about being noisy. But she's right.

"I do have a stealth mode for the HeliBoaJee. It takes more fuel, so we can't use it for too long. For now I'll turn it on."

The sounds we heard earlier were coming from the northwest, so I start us moving in that direction. The screen continues to show pictures without any sign of Rafi or the loggers.

"Hold on," I say. "We're on the edge of a clearing. Looks like a small camp down there, maybe where they sleep at night. I'm going to circle around, but we've got to stay far enough back that those guys can't see us, if they happen to be home."

"Sure hope Rafi's not down there," Stowe mutters.

She angles the scope out into the open area and keeps taking pictures. At first it's too small to make out. But I glance at the frames on the screen, coming from the loggers' camp. "Wow, what is that?"

"Rafi?" Stowe whips her head up to see what's on the screen.

"No, but maybe something else we're looking for."

14. CAGES

S towe slides the screen toward her and zooms in to get a closer look. "Whoa, Wig, those look like baby orangutans in cages—two of them. These guys are not just illegal loggers—they're poachers too!"

I take a quick look at the images. "Sure looks like it. Do you think one of those babies is Buddi?"

"Should we send the Finder down to check?" Stowe asks.

"Maybe not. No sign of the loggers, but they could be back anytime now. Let's hope without Rafi in a cage. We don't want them to capture the Finder, or even worse, figure out we've seen the orangutans."

"Good point. Don't you think we should call Ariella and Angga, and tell them Rafi's missing?" Stowe's brow wrinkles and her mouth turns down.

"I don't know. They can't help, and they'll go crazy. Let's give ourselves a little more time to find him first."

"All right. Any ideas how to do that?"

"Let's start by getting away from the camp," I suggest. "Then we'll risk searching with the Finder. Could you bring Rafi's gear over here?"

As we fly away, Stowe uses the vacuum system to pull Rafi's scent out of his backpack and into the Finder.

"Thanks," I say. "Our pup's ready to go hunting." I'd give our bionic dog a pat, but I better keep my hands on the flight controls.

"Now, where should we start?"

"Good news is, Rafi's on foot so he can't have gotten that far from where we left him," Stowe says.

"Let's hope the chainsaw guys got tired of looking for him." Otherwise the bad news will be—Rafi's on foot.

Hoping for the best, and not having a better plan, I fly us back to the air space above the site of our earlier mishap.

The area below is quiet, like when we first arrived. No sign of the loggers.

As we hover, Stowe programs the Finder, and sends our drone down to a few feet above the ground.

We stare at the monitor as our puppy scopes things out. "Looks like it's picked up Rafi's scent," I say, as we watch it twirl around at the spot where our vehicle got stuck. Then it whips around and zips over to the giant fig tree Rafi climbed earlier when he tied up the HeliBoaJee.

"What's it doing now?" Stowe asks, as the Finder stops and turns 90 degrees. It heads straight up the tree trunk and out onto the limb where Rafi was perched when he saw the approaching loggers. It wobbles around, almost like a person trying to keep his balance. And then it dives down the side of a thick, ropy looking vine. "Wow, look at that thing go!"

The Finder heads toward a nearby stream, where it starts to spin in place. "Rafi must have gone into the water." Good plan if you don't want to leave tracks. Not so helpful for us.

"Time for you to direct the search," I tell Stowe. She guides the Finder, back and forth across the stream.

"It reminds me of a pond skater, you know, those bugs that hunt by skimming across the water," Stowe says, her eyes glued to the monitor. "Come on, pick up Rafi's scent."

"At some point Rafi must have left the water. Why don't you move the Finder up onto land and let it take control again," I suggest to Stowe.

Off it goes, bounding along the water's edge in a west/ northwest direction. "Yes! It's picked up something."

We've been searching for over an hour, and covered a few miles. Rafi must be running.

"Look," Stowe shouts, handing me her binoculars. "I see him!"

"Yup, there's our fearless guide. Let's hurry up and get on the ground."

Stowe hardly waits for the blades to stop before she jumps out. "We are sooo glad to see you."

"Sorry we left without you," I say, joining them. It is a relief to be together again.

"Hey, man, no worries. I told you to go. It was easier escaping on my own," Rafi says, with a twinkle in his eyes.

"According to our Finder you must have propelled out of the tree on one of those giant vines and run through the stream." Stowe sounds breathless describing what she thinks happened.

"Pretty close," Rafi confirms. "The part your Finder missed was the two guys chasing me."

"But you escaped." I guess he is a child of the rainforest.

"Yeah. How'd you do it?" Stowe says, in a voice a little too high pitched.

She doesn't need to go overboard. Rafi did get away.

"The loggers saw me same time I spied them. They figured they got me, since I was up in the tree. Too bad, I noticed that there were many vines wrapped around the tree. Not sure what you call them in English, we call them *rotan.*"

"There is something called a rattan palm. I think it's a thorny vine?" Stowe does know some random stuff.

"Anyway, there were these rattan palms laying on the branches. Good thing my knife not in my backpack with you guys," he says, patting his pocket.

"Look what the thorns have done to your hands," Stowe gasps. Rafi has big gashes on his palms and across his knuckles.

Nurse Stowe grabs the first aid kit. "Here, let me help you clean those up."

"No worries. Not so bad," Rafi says, reaching for some gauze and bandaids.

It's obvious he can take care of his own medical needs.

"And the vines saved you how?" I ask. Let's get back to the story.

"I cut vines, and grabbed one for my escape. Just before I swung out of tree, I sent the other vines right down on loggers' heads. They had to take time undoing them, otherwise they get ripped up. While they were busy, I hit the ground and ran."

"I don't want to see those dudes again, but I hope their whole bodies look like your hands." I guess this is the new me. I don't usually want to see blood on anybody.

"Speaking of the loggers, before we rescued you," I say, giving Rafi a little jab, "we saw something pretty interesting at their camp."

"You went to logger camp alone? You guys crazy?"

"No, we aren't that dumb—"

Stowe interrupts me, and tells Rafi about the Binocula-ser, and how we saw the caged orangutans, and our theory that one of them is Buddi.

"Hmm. Good guess, since we know Buddi nested in the area.

"Not sure what that means. The loggers are poachers, but I do not think they are ones who will move these animals out of Borneo." Rafi scratches his head.

"We were wondering too," Stowe says.

"More likely," Rafi continues, "these guys are—I think word is—middlemen. They found the orangutans, shot the mothers, and grabbed the babies. Those guys must know some wildlife traffickers out here."

Stowe gives the two of us her intense eyeball-to-eyeball stare. "We need a rescue plan, and quick, before the really bad guys get a hold of the babies."

15. Low On Fuel

"We used some extra methane when I put us in stealth mode looking for you," I tell Rafi. "Before we get back to searching for the babies, the HeliBoaJee needs to be refueled or we're going to get into worse trouble."

"I understand," Rafi says. "We are close to the park boundary, where there is a peat swamp in wooded area next to some farmland. It is only another few miles."

"Okay. Let's go." We all climb back into the HeliBoaJee and take off.

Stowe tells Rafi about the call from his father.

He rolls his eyes. "We all need the same story. You said I was looking for refueling spot, right?"

We nod. I sure hope Ariella doesn't find out what happened. And when do we tell them about the baby sightings?

Rafi's been keeping his eye on the horizon. "Touch down over there." He points. "But make sure you are out from under trees. We do not need to get stuck again."

I land us on firm ground *close* to the peat swamp.

Stowe looks around. "That's odd—cleared land right next to the rain forest."

"You thank the farmers. They came from other islands in Indonesia, cut down trees and drained bogs."

While Stowe and Rafi are discussing history, I've gone to work setting up the methane concentrator. "If I can interrupt your conversation, we've got to get cracking. Rafi, do me a favor, grab the two gas tanks strapped under the HeliBoaJee."

"We're going to pull air from the bog through this," I explain, pointing at a long, steel canister. "It's packed with a special material that adsorbs and concentrates methane."

"Stowe, you keep an eye on the concentrator gauge. As soon as the canister is full, hook up the first gas tank and the methane will discharge into it. Then reconnect the tank to the HeliBoaJee, and I'll get the next one hooked up."

"Got it, Dr. Hot Air. How long's this going to take? Do we need to be worried about the loggers finding us?"

"It'll take about an hour to refuel. The process is pretty quiet, and all the forest sounds should muffle the noise of the machine. Rafi, do you think the guys are still out there looking for you?"

He shrugs. "Maybe I discourage them with my escape. But keep your voice down." He makes a note of the time on his phone.

"And you're sure there's enough methane to fill our tanks?" That's Stowe, always doubting me.

"Oh yeah. There's tons. Way more than we need." I rev up the motor to start sucking air out of the bog.

When the meter hits full, I point to my cousin. Off she goes with the first tank, while jabbering into her headset. We've been so busy there hasn't been much time to dictate logs.

Stowe straps the first tank back on the HeliBoaJee and grabs Ariella's camera. "I saw some pitcher plants over there," she points. "Got to take a look."

"Do _not_ get stuck, whatever you do," I warn.

"Aye, aye, Captain," she salutes.

Rafi laughs. "You guys are funny. Wheaton, this refueling idea, it is amazing. Great use for methane. Better than adding carbon that goes straight into the air. You are a real engineer, man."

"Yeah, guess I am. And what about you? Are you going to be a forest ranger like your father?"

"No. The work my father does is important. But I have other ideas what I want to do with my future."

"Like what?" I ask.

"I love to draw. My parents say I make no money as an artist, and they want me to be a doctor. But my dream is to move to Yogyakarta—"

"Where's that?" I interrupt.

"It is on another Indonesian island called Java. My mother is not happy about me moving away..."

"Yeah, tell me about it." I sure get that problem. "But what's so special about this Yogi place?"

"There is a good Art Institute where I can study to become a painter. Lots of artist live in that city. My dream is to open a studio someday."

"What kinds of stuff do you paint?"

Rafi pulls out his cell phone. I notice he glances at the time and kind of looks around before bringing up his pictures.

"Don't worry, we're almost done," I assure him.

He nods, and then passes me his phone. "A painting I did of a pygmy elephant and its baby."

This guy's really good.

"Hey Stowe, get over here. You have to see this."

Our resident photographer comes bounding back. "I just shot photos of some tiny pitcher plants. They're green and they grow on vines so I didn't even have to step on the bog." She winks.

"Awesome. Now check out Rafi's art work." I pass Rafi's phone to Stowe.

"Wow, this is incredible. Have you seen one of these elephants live?" Stowe is beaming.

"Oh, yes. One time I help my father conduct a census of them. I took a bunch of pictures, and then worked on the painting at school. Won first prize in competition."

Rafi's not showing off now. You can tell this is important to him.

"Ariella's a famous wildlife photographer. You should show her some of your stuff," I suggest. It's hard living in a kid's body, when you can do grown-up stuff.

Time to get back on track. "Good news. I think we're all tanked up." And so far no visitors.

As we get ready to climb into the HeliBoaJee we see a motorcycle cruising our way. "Oh no, more trouble?" I look at Rafi, but he's already walking toward the oncoming vehicle.

STOWE LEBLOND'S LOG

Borneo, Indonesia

April 11

5:00 PM

We've seen a lot of the tropical rain forest today. It is awesome.

There are so many different trees that make up this forest. A really cool one is the ironwood, or as the Indonesians call it belian. Some of these trees can live 1,000 years. They grow very slowly. You measure tree growth by figuring out the diameter of the tree at chest height. For belian, the annual growth rate is about 0.023 inches/year. That is s-l-o-w. Red maple grows about 0.3 inches/year – more than 10 times as fast. Because the belian is such a slow grower, it's really dense – that means it's heavy! You know how when trees are harvested in New England, sometimes they're sent down the river as floating logs? Well, the logs of belian are so heavy that they sink. Loggers need to strap them to rafts made from less dense logs, when they're transporting them on the water. I think we saw some on our way into the park.

We're learning a lot about peat swamps on this trip! They feel like a squooshy mess when you walk on them. Some peat swamps started forming after the last ice age – that's 12,000 years ago. What happens in some places is that the leaves fall and trees die, but the ground gets flooded. When the leaves are in a lot of water, the oxygen from the air can't get to them. Over time the bogs get packed down with all these *leaves and plant material. Some of these bogs in Borneo can be up to 20 meters deep. That's almost 66 feet! Yikes.*

MATH PROBLEM:

1 meter = 3.28 feet

20 meters X 3.28 = 65.6 feet

Usually microorganisms break down leaves on the forest floor, but since there is so little oxygen in this water/leaf mixture, there are only a small number of microbes that can do the job. They are anaerobic, which means they work without oxygen. When these anaerobes break down the leaf tissue, one of the main gases that comes off is methane.

Now take the methane from the bogs, and add in what's emitted from using natural gas, and burning vegetation, and put it together with the carbon dioxide belched into our atmosphere, and the earth's got a big problem.

When the earth absorbs sunlight, it reflects infrared light back out into the atmosphere. The carbon dioxide and methane absorb the infrared light, forming a blanket of warm air around the earth. The result is climate change, which means melting icebergs, increases in storms, and droughts!

We're using the methane from the bogs to fuel the HeliBoaJee. Since methane causes much more warming than carbon dioxide, it's good to use it for fuel instead of letting it creep into the environment.

WORDS I'M LEARNING IN INDONESIAN:

Ibu – mother

Bayi – baby

Sampaijumpalagi – see you later

Selamatjalan – goodbye (when you are leaving)

Rotan – rattan palm (I think the word for palm is Te-lapk, but Rafi calls these plants rotan)

16. The Longhouse

The motorcycle stops in front of Rafi. A man and a boy hop off, and the three of them start talking. The man is in work pants and a short-sleeved blue shirt. Isn't dressed like a logger. The boy, who looks like he's about Rafi's age, has a red bandana around his head, and is wearing a white t-shirt with a cool insignia that looks like a purple house with a fish on top of it. Says *Persipura*. Maybe they run a fish restaurant. It's getting close to dinnertime, and the idea of eating sounds good to me.

The man puts his hand on Rafi's shoulder and then pulls out his cell phone.

"Do you think there's service here?" Wheaton says.

"The guy's laying his hands on Rafi, and you're wondering if our phones will work? Do you think we need to get out of here?" Stowe hisses.

"Not sure. Before, Rafi did yell for us to leave. This time he's looking at the ground. Doesn't seem like he's getting ready to run."

The man starts talking in a loud voice. Then he starts laughing and hands the phone to Rafi.

There's a lot of conversation but it's all in Indonesian.

"I think he said *Ayah*," Stowe says. "Maybe that guy knows Angga?"

Rafi hangs up.

"Come over," he gestures. "Meet my uncle Farhan and cousin Halim."

Then Rafi says a bunch more to them. I hear him say Wheaton Guinto and Stowe LeBlond. He must be explaining who we are.

"So do they own a restaurant or something?" I point at Halim's shirt.

"Ha, no. Uncle Farhan is a farmer. My cousin wearing a soccer shirt—*Persipura*—an important team in Indonesia."

"I play a little soccer," Stowe says, kicking her foot to demonstrate.

Sports are the next best thing to knowing a foreign language, I guess.

"Rafi, did you just talk to your father?" I'm dreading the answer. We were supposed to call quite a while ago.

"Yeah. He and Ariella are displeased with us for being out of touch for so long—again."

"What did you tell them?" Stowe asks, her eyebrows rising.

"Did you tell them we may have found Buddi?" I whisper. Not sure why, since it doesn't seem like his uncle and cousin understand English.

"No. And I left out the stuff about the loggers. I only told them we had a little trouble getting the HeliBoaJee unstuck, but we are fine now. And I mentioned we refueled."

"Did he believe you?"

"Who knows?" Rafi shrugs. "But he and my uncle both said we must stop for tonight. It will be dark soon—"

"It's only 5:30 PM." Stowe interrupts. "And we need to get to the babies before the traffickers do."

"I know, but we are in the tropics, not far from the equator. The sun set at 6:00 PM and will not rise for 12 hours.

"Uncle Farhan invite us to spend the night with them, and my father and Ariella said we accept the invitation. They stopped for the day too. Ariella, my father and Bella are staying at nearby research station with some scientists in the area. I was *told* we all start out again in the morning."

Halim can't take his eyes off the HeliBoaJee.

"Come on over," I say, waving for the boy to climb in and take a look. Farhan joins him.

"How far is their farm from here?" I ask Rafi.

"Close by, but I think Halim would love to come for a ride. Okay, Wheaton?"

"Sure, as long as you can get us there without any more detours." I flash him a grin.

Rafi tells his uncle that we will take Halim and meet him in a few minutes.

We get back in the HeliBoaJee, and I do a quick flyover around the perimeter of the family's coconut farm. As soon as we land, a woman in a flowered shirt and skirt comes over to greet us.

"*Halo*, Bibi Gita." Rafi leans over and gives her a kiss. "And there is Hana." He blows a kiss and waves to a little girl peeking out the door of a long wooden house, sitting on stilts. I guess flooding is a problem.

Rafi and his aunt proceed to have a conversation. Uncle Farhan and Halim join in.

"Aunt Gita is so happy to meet you," Rafi tells us. "Let us grab our things and head inside. We eat soon."

Climbing up into the house, we make our way down a narrow hall to the guest room, where we toss our backpacks onto the bunk beds. Then it's across the way to the kitchen and family area, to join everyone for the evening meal. I'm not quite sure what to expect.

Aunt Gita brings out hot steaming rice and a big dish of something that doesn't look at all familiar.

"Oh wow, is this *tahutelor*? I've wanted to try this," Stowe says, sounding very sincere.

Aunt Gita nods and smiles. Rafi winks and gives his head a positive shake too.

I look at Stowe. "Translate."

"It's a deep-fried bean curd omelet, and you dip it in that peanut sauce," she says, pointing at one of the small bowls at each of our places.

Okay... here goes. I follow Stowe's instructions, dipping a piece of the brown greasy thing in the sauce, and popping it into my mouth. Mmm, it's good. Can't decide if it tastes like French fries or crispy chicken skin.

When we're done eating the main meal, Hana turns to Rafi.

"*Ayo makan kelapa.*"

"Hana wants you to have a *kelapa*, a coconut, for desert."

All I can remember is my mother's warning about eating anything that hasn't been cooked, unless it's been washed and peeled with a clean knife. But we can't embarrass our host.

I turn to Rafi. "I have a surprise for the kids. Could you ask them to meet us out back with a few large bowls of water? I'll also need a machete, or whatever you typically use to cut coconuts." Time for a Wheaton-technology/magic show.

I run to our room and grab my laser-sterilizer. The kids bring down the water as requested, and lead us to a huge penned-in area behind the house filled with coconuts from the recent harvest. Hana picks out the biggest one she can carry and brings it to us.

"Rafi, please translate as I demonstrate." Then I turn to my audience.

"I have here a magic laser. Do not look at the laser as it can hurt your eyes. Just watch what it does." I aim the laser at the water in the glass. In a matter of seconds it comes to a boil. Hana squeals, and claps her hands.

We wait a few minutes for the water to cool. "Now for the magic wash," I say, pouring some of the sterilized liquid over the coconut, careful to cover every spot. "Rafi, dip the machete in the remaining water and be sure to shake the blade ten times. The magic water will make this machete the sharpest ever."

With more dramatic flair than I would have guessed, Rafi begins to wash the knife while getting his little cousin to count.

"Satu, dua, tiga, empat, lima, enam, tuju, delapan, sembilan, sepuluh."

With the magic wash completed, we split open the coconut, drain the milk and cut the flesh up for everyone to enjoy.

Little Hana says something and giggles.

"She said this magic coconut the best she ever had! Good job, Wheaton. Thanks for not telling Hana you worry about bacteria in the water out here," Rafi whispers to me.

I can feel my face turning red, and am glad when Stowe changes the subject. "I've wanted to ask you this all day," she says, pointing at Rafi's shirt. "Who's Saptarasa?"

"Who Saptarasa? The coolest band around. Here, listen." He finds a YouTube link on his phone.

I glance up at the satellite dish on the Rezaputra roof. This place just got a little closer to home.

With the volume turned up, a band starts up. Rafi and Halim play air guitar and keyboard, mouthing words that sound like English. With the drums beating in the background, Hana begins to dance and Stowe pops up to join her. "Come on, Wheaton," she says, holding out her hand to me.

"No thanks, I'll take a video to show Ariella." I whip out my phone and start recording. No way I'm dancing.

After a few rounds of the YouTube, Stowe turns to Rafi.

"Before we go to bed, don't you think we better plan how we're going to rescue the babies tomorrow?"

"Not now," he says giving her an intense stare. "Good night."

Hmmm. What was all that about? We're pretty tired, so I'm not going to ask. I pick up my "magic" equipment, and the two of us head to our bedroom.

As we reach the guest quarters my cell phone vibrates. HOW ARE YOU DOING? EATING ENOUGH? GETTING ANY REST? MOM.

I show my phone to Stowe. "It's the start of their day at home. We better send some texts. Keep it simple and uninformative," I tell my cousin. "Like, we're safe, all's going well, more detail tomorrow. Don't have to say Ariella's someplace else."

"Or mention what happened with the loggers," Stowe mumbles.

We both get going on our texting.

As Stowe hears the swish of the send, she hops onto the top bunk. "I'll be quiet soon, but I need to work on my log for a few."

For the first time all day I relax, listening to Stowe blabbing into her headset. But then there's a knock at the door.

STOWE LEBLOND'S LOG

Borneo, Indonesia

April 11

8:00 PM

Tonight we're guests of Farhan Rezaputra, the brother of Angga the forest ranger who brought us to Borneo. Farhan lives on a coconut farm with his wife Gita, their teenage son, Halim and little daughter Hana. She's soooo cute.

Coconut palms originated in Indonesia, but because they can float, they travel thousands of miles around the globe. When they wash up somewhere else in the world, they're still alive to grow a new tree. Guess that's how they ended up in North America. In fertile soil one tree can produce as many as 75 coconuts. Most farms in Borneo don't have the best soil, so trees only produce around 30 each. Coconut is used in a lot of Indonesian cooking, and nothing is wasted, from the white flesh to the milk pressed out of it. Even the husks are used. I think that's what Ariella's front doormat is made of.

Farhan's family has a nice garden where they grow all the rice they need for the year, bananas and some other fruits that are a big part of their diet. Reminds me of our garden except that we have potatoes and kale.

The family home is built in the longhouse style, developed by the Dayaks, the native people of Borneo. You may have guessed, the houses are very long ☺. They sit on stilts to protect against flooding. Years ago many families lived in one longhouse. All the private "apartments" for each family were on one side of the hall, protected from bad weather. The guest rooms were on the other side, along with common spaces for activities like drying rice. Today, families like Farhan's build homes using the same style, but only for one family. In the old days people sometimes kept their animals under the longhouses. But Farhan and Gita's chickens are in a pen away from the house—a good idea. Mom, remember how the chickens smelled when we use to keep them behind our house?

WORDS I'M LEARNING IN INDONESIAN:

Bibi – Aunt

Kelapa – coconut

pencuci mulut – dessert

Satu, dua, tiga, empat, lima, enam, tuju, delapan, sembilan, sepuluh – now I can count from one through ten!

17. LOGGERS' CAMP

"It's us," a voice hisses from the other side of the door.

I open up and see Rafi and Halim. They're wearing cargo pants and long-sleeved shirts, with bandanas on their heads. I doubt those are Indonesian pajamas.

"Get Stowe. We go after babies tonight," Rafi orders.

"Is that a good idea?" All I can remember is that the loggers are probably the ones who shot Bella. What is Rafi thinking?

Stowe hears us and appears at the doorway, her head set propped up like a crown. "What's up?"

"Here is the problem," Rafi says. "No way loggers will hold on to babies for long. They need to be fed. Not something those guys do. Young orangutan are not worth one rupiah dead. I worry they will try and sell them soon."

"You almost got caught this afternoon. How are we going to do this, and not end up in cages hanging from trees ourselves?" There goes my leg.

"Wheaton, come on. You have that *mufflizer* thing for the HeliBoaJee, and night vision goggles. And now there are four of us. We can so do it." Stowe may have circles under her eyes, but her rapid-fire speech doesn't sound like someone ready to go to sleep.

"Here is my plan," Rafi begins. "We fly back to the spot where you landed HeliBoaJee last time. Okay, not exact spot, but close." He flashes me a grin.

"Remember how you marked trees with red X's? That will help us move in right direction. When we find logger camp, we grab babies and be back before anyone misses us."

"Won't the little orangutans make noise and give us away?" Glad Stowe's starting to think ahead.

Halim smiles and holds up a jar of honey. "This favorite treat for them. We squeeze some in cages, and they too busy to complain."

"You speak English?" Stowe's eyebrows arch.

"Yeah. But don't worry. My father—not a word." Halim winks at us.

These cousins seem to have all the answers. "Okay, I guess we have a plan." I sure hope Rafi knows what he's doing.

Stowe and I get back into our field clothes and grab our backpacks. The four of us creep across the yard. The insect symphony coming from the nearby rainforest drowns out the sound of our shoes crunching on the ground.

We climb into the HeliBoaJee.

"I think we better drive away and then lift off. It'll be quieter, so we won't disturb your parents' sleep," I say, looking straight at Halim.

Before long we're back at the edge of the forest. "Hang on," I tell the others, as I convert our vehicle back into helicopter mode. "Buckle up."

As we lift off I glance back at the farm. A light goes on. No reason to point this out to the others. Maybe someone in the house had to go to the bathroom.

"Stowe, if you look at the flight history—" I point at a tab on the computer screen "—it'll give you the coordinates of our earlier locations. Find our first stop near the bog."

"Got it," she says, and begins giving me navigational cues for our flight path.

In no time, she reports, "Okay, we're near the landing spot."

Before setting us down, I turn to the team. "Things are going to quiet down. But don't worry. I'm putting us into stealth mode—"

"He means he's turning on the mufflizer." Good old Stowe, the translator.

"One more thing," Stowe stays, "*Stay off the bog.*"

With a little more "help" from Stowe, I get us landed. We agree that Rafi and I will wear the night goggles, with Halim and Stowe following close behind. No headlamps to attract attention.

That smell we picked up when we landed at the park earlier in the day is ten times more intense tonight. It feels a little like visiting a botanical garden conservatory in the middle of the summer. Glad the night goggles have an anti-fogging treatment or they wouldn't be worth much.

"Few spots still there," Rafi says, pointing to traces of the earlier markings on the trees.

We walk along for a while, when Rafi holds up his hand and points north.

"Is that the camp?" Stowe sounds breathless, and I feel like my legs might give out.

Rafi nods. "Let us see how things look."

The four of us walk toward the clearing. Each footstep seems to groan as our hiking shoes make contact with the soft, moist ground.

"Wow, they've cleared out acres, I mean hectares, of rainforest." Stowe's angry voice is a little above a whisper. Halim puts his finger to his lips.

"Wonder where the loggers are sleeping. Or if they're sleeping at all?" I sure hope Rafi knows what he's doing.

We continue to walk the perimeter of the logging site. When you're in the rain forest, you shouldn't be able to see the sky, but with the canopy cut down, we get glimpses of the moon, playing hide-and-seek with the clouds.

"Check it out, guys," Rafi whispers, pointing about 25 feet from where we're standing. "There they are."

Two cages hang from branches of one of the belian trees the loggers haven't gotten around to chopping down yet.

"Can you see, are the babies asleep? Are they okay?" Stowe is getting revved up again.

"Here. Take a look." Rafi hands her the night goggles.

"Yup, they're resting. And I suppose their keepers are also down for the night," Stowe says, pointing to a pop-up tent not far from the prize orangutans.

"Surprised there are no fences here?" I mutter under my breath.

"Loggers keep moving through rain forest as they harvest trees. Lucky no dog." Halim has been around this world for a long time, I guess.

"This what we are going to do," Rafi tells us. "Wheaton, you wait back here with Stowe. Halim and I are taller. Let us grab cages.

"Take goggles from Stowe. I will walk behind you," he orders his cousin. "And make sure you have honey ready."

Halim nods.

"We will be back fast, and then need to get out of here before the loggers discover what happened."

Rafi makes it sound simple, but nothing's ever that easy.

Stowe and I stand close together and watch as the cousins make their way forward. They are about ten feet from the babies when a siren goes off.

"*Ambilbayi*," Rafi yells, "*dan pergi.*" Then he says some other stuff but all I catch is HeliBoaJee.

Halim looks at his cousin for a split second and nods. Then he grabs the cages and sprints in our direction.

"Why isn't Rafi running too?" Stowe hisses at me.

A powerful light, mounted on a nearby tree, turns on, and two men emerge from the camper. They still look like wrestling champs. We watch as our fearless leader stands with his back to the pickup truck hunched over like he's got something under his arms. They start hollering at Rafi as he takes off, but in the opposite direction from us. The loggers follow, and they're running fast.

"He's diverting them." I whisper.

By now Halim has rejoined us with his precious cargo. "Rafi said we take the orangutan and get out of here. He meet us back at the HeliBoaJee."

No way we can abandon him.

"Halim, you still have a pair of night goggles, right? You and Stowe take the cages and get going. I'll wait to be sure Rafi's safe. Don't worry, I'll catch up." My leg is no longer shaking, even though my heart is pounding like the drums in Rafi's music.

The two of them stand still for a second. "Beat it," I say. "*Pergi!*" Not sure what that means but it does the trick. They take off.

Halim and Stowe seem to be running in the wrong direction too, but I don't dare call out, as they disappear into the forest.

For a few minutes it's very still. But then I hear those guys screaming again. And now I see them dragging Rafi back toward the camp.

18. FLIGHT

C rouching behind a rock, I watch through my night goggles, praying the loggers don't see me.

One of the guys has a tattoo of a snake on his arm, the one that's pinned across Rafi's body.

The other man's skinny, but you can see his muscles bulging, almost like Popeye in the cartoon.

He's headed to the tent. Must have realized he's running around in his underwear and flip flops.

A few minutes later the logger is back wearing cargo pants and a black t-shirt with a skull and crossbones on it. Now he's got on what look like soccer cleats. More important, he's carrying a rope.

The guys tie up Rafi's hands and feet, and scream something at him. I can only guess what they're saying, but it can't be good. They shove him to the ground and start to run in my direction.

Skull and Crossbones stops, holds up his hand, and takes out what looks like a remote. He points at a tree to their left, and clicks in the direction where the lowest branch emerges from the trunk. Then he does the same to the right. The air becomes very still. The screaming alarm has stopped. He gestures, and the two of them walk a few paces. Then he seems to repeat the process. He's turning the alarm back on.

My heart hasn't slowed down. If they discover me, I'm sure they'll find more rope. But then they look down on the ground and give each other a fist bump. From where I'm standing, it looks like they've found Halim and Stowe's footprints. They turn and take off following the path made by our cousins. This is not going to be good.

I wait until the loggers are out of earshot. "Rafi, are you okay?"

"Do I look okay?" he hisses. "Come and untie me."

"I can't. Don't you realize what's going on here?" Rafi may know this forest, but he has a lot to learn about technology. "They have an invisible optical fence, controlled by units in the trees. When you and Halim ran through it, the beam was disrupted, sounding the alarm."

"So I just wait for them to come back here?" For the first time Rafi doesn't sound so brave.

"Nooo. Hold on." I dig into my backpack and pull out my laser sterilizer. "I have a high energy channel on this thing that should be able to disengage the sensors."

Pretty sure I saw where Skull and Crossbones pointed when he reactivated the sensors. "Here we go." As I zap each, I think of those heist movies where the thief disables the security system protecting jewels on display in a museum.

"Are you sure it is okay to walk in here?" Rafi still hasn't gotten his confidence back.

"Hope so, because here I come."

With my eyes squinting and teeth clenched, I cross the zone of the invisible fence. When no siren goes off, my breathing starts up again. I race over and with my hands still shaking, I struggle to loosen the knots that grip Rafi's wrists.

"Thanks, man. Let's go."

"I'm worried," I say. "The guys followed Stowe and Halim's tracks."

"I saw that too. But the footsteps did not go in the direction of HeliBoaJee?"

"And that's a good thing?"

"I think so. We should go straight back to our vehicle," Rafi suggests. "If they are not there, we start looking for them."

With the help of the night goggles, I find the marks on the trees one more time. As we make our way back, we hear voices shouting in the distance.

"Can you tell who's yelling?"

"Not sure," Rafi says as we arrive at the HeliBoaJee. "The voices not either of our cousins. I wish Stowe and Halim were waiting for us." He looks worried.

"Do you think they were captured? What should we do?"

"Wait a minute," Rafi says, pulling his cell phone from his pocket. "Text from Halim. He says, AHEAD OF LOGGERS, BUT THEY R HOT ON TRAIL. WHERE R U?"

Rafi texts back. WE R @HeliBoaJee. His phone buzzes again.

COMING. B READY 2 LIFT OFF.

I get everything set for departure but keep the engine off. No point in announcing our location to the loggers.

We peer out into the darkness from our HeliBoaJee hideaway. I've got my night goggles on, but no sign of Stowe's yellow curls. Voices seem to be coming in our direction. But not the ones we want to hear.

There's a rustling sound on the ground. "Oh no," I say turning to Rafi.

But then we catch a glimpse of two familiar figures, bounding toward us.

"They're not carrying the cages anymore. Must have lost the babies." Not sure I care. I'm so relieved to see them.

"No, they have them," Rafi says, pointing at two hairy balls gripping Stowe's and Halim's chests.

Our cousins climb up into the HeliBoaJee with their passengers clinging tight.

"Get going," Stowe says. "Here they come."

I turn on the engine and pull up. Looking down, we can see the loggers coming into view, carrying the empty metal cages. But we've passed through the window in the trees, and those goons can't see us anymore.

"Whoa! That was something," Stowe says, high fiving with Halim.

"Yeah, we were worried. You guys went in the wrong direction."

"Not really." Stowe explains. "It was Halim's idea for us to confuse the loggers by starting out the way we did."

"We had weight problem. The babies are light. Big one weighs five kilograms and this other one less," Halim tells us.

"Five kilograms is around eleven pounds," Stowe lets me know.

"Thanks. I am familiar with the metric system." Maybe she's forgotten. I'm a college grad.

"No way we escape fast carrying these little orangutans in cages. They were heavy to carry." Halim imitates what it looked like to be weighed down by those clunky carriers.

"But how did you get the babies to go to you?" My brother sure wouldn't go to a stranger.

"It was a little bit of a challenge, especially with the smaller one," Stowe tells us. "They weren't that excited about coming to us at first—"

Halim jumps into the conversation. "Maybe they saw humans shooting their mothers. But not much time for us to make friends."

"So we poured honey on our fingers, and rubbed it on the babies' lips." Stowe smiles. "Their little tongues went into action and they were ours."

Halim points to their shoulders where the babies are now lapping away. "We poured more honey on our shoulder and the two jumped in our arms like we were best friend."

"Anyway, we threw the cages off into swampy area and doubled back, walking on logs for a while. Harder to track us." Halim looks at Stowe, who is nodding. "Loggers figure out what we were doing. We hear them getting closer. But they stop to pull orangutan prisons out of swamp. They need them for future captives."

Now its Rafi's turn to explain how I sprung him. "Wheaton has a lot of tricks in that backpack."

No more time for reviewing the evening's adventures. We're back at the farm, and it's already 5:00 AM.

"It will be light in one hour," Rafi reminds us. "Let's take the babies to your room before anyone wakes up."

19. Returning To The Farm

We creep back up the stairs to our room, the four of us and our baby orangutans.

Stowe flops down on the floor. "Before I forget, I'm keeping a little dictionary of Indonesian words we're learning. What did you mean when you said *ambilbayi* and *dan pergi*? I know *bayi* is babies but guessed at the rest."

Rafi smiles. "You don't miss much. *Ambilbayi* means 'take the babies' and *dan pergi* means 'and go'. No reason you need to repeat those phrases around our family."

I nod in agreement. "Glad I used *pergi* correctly back there at the loggers' camp."

While we're getting a lesson in Indonesian the babies have been getting comfortable. They're like little kids, each with its own personality. The bigger of the two is red-haired, just like Bella. He starts exploring right away and starts swinging from the cord of the window shade. Guess it reminds him of a vine. The little one has much darker hair. He watches for a while, but then he gets into the act, climbing up on our bunk bed and leaping down. It doesn't take long before they knock over a lamp and start making some rather loud chirping sounds.

"Shsh," I say.

"Really, Wheaton, that's going to do a lot." Stowe turns to the Rezaputra boys. "We better find a way to keep these fellas quiet for a while, or they'll wake up your family. Do you have any old baby bottles around? Maybe we could give them something to drink?"

"Halim, get some old bottle from your sister, and fill with water." Then Rafi turns to us. "These two are one-year-olds, so they can eat fruits–"

"We have star fruit," I say.

"We had some." Stowe looks down.

"Figures you'd eat the good stuff. I'm sure we still have some durian. Stowe wouldn't have eaten any of that!"

"Good idea. You did not bring them up here?" Halim laughs and holds his nose.

"Right about that. I'll run back to the HeliBoaJee and grab the bag," Stowe says, racing out the door before I can bug her about hogging all the star fruit.

I sure hope she's quiet. We still have to figure out how to explain these little ones when Halim's parents wake up.

"I go get them a coconut too," Halim suggests. "They old enough to eat some."

Stowe comes back with the durian. The little guys start pointing and jumping, even before they can see the special delivery.

"Yuck. I guess one person's vomit smell is another's yummy aroma."

"That's one way to put it," Stowe says, shaking her head at me.

Rafi pulls out his knife and slices the fruits in half. Each baby gets some, and they dive in. Good news, they finish it all up, so we won't have to take any with us.

Halim reappears with a coconut and a couple of bottles filled with water.

"Here you go, little guys," I say, holding the bottles up for them. They look perplexed, but after a couple of minutes they catch on. One starts sucking on the nipple, and the other one follows suit.

Meanwhile, Halim takes the coconut and smashes it open with a machete. So much for being quiet. Next thing we know the door to our room opens. It's Uncle Farhan.

"Hmphh," he utters, giving me a strange look.

Wonder if he was the one going to the bathroom last night?

Uncle Farhan kneels down on the floor and looks closely at the two baby orangutans, and then says something to his son.

Halim is staring at the ground. "My father said there are a few new guests since last night."

Stowe and I look at each other. No way this is going to go well for any of us.

There's a lot of back and forth, and some hand waving. Finally Uncle Farhan shakes his head and says a few more things, before he gets up and walks out of the room. The door swings a little too wide, and slams a little too hard.

"What did you say?" I ask.

Halim laughs a little. "We told truth, but left out few things. My dad will call Angga and Ariella to tell them what is happening."

"That's going to be fun. *Not*," I say, looking at Stowe, who's gritting her teeth.

She rolls her eyes and nods.

"My father have a good question." Halim continues. "We sure one of these babies is Buddi? And which one? They both males."

"I wondered that too," I say, "but figured, whoever's babies they are, they don't deserve to be in cages. We can answer the question about Buddi. I'll be right back."

I race to the HeliBoaJee and grab the Finder. Once back up in our room, I dial the Finder back to the scent we got off Bella's clean leg. Nothing happens. Then I tune to the channel with Buddi and Bella's smells from the hammock, and let our bionic dog sniff around the two babies. It moves close to the larger red-haired one, and the Finder starts spinning. "Bingo, that's Bella's boy!"

"And who do you belong to?" Stowe coos to the other little orangutan.

"That is a question my father may answer," Rafi says. "He, or wildlife ecologist out here, may know of other mothers and their offspring who disappeared.

"And when we talk to my father and Ariella," Rafi takes a deep breath, "we better all have same story about last night. We have to be truthful about going out to rescue little guys, but Halim did not tell my uncle about me being captured, or how Wheaton helped with escape. No need to share that stuff."

We all nod in agreement.

"Speaking of the little ones," Stowe points to our babies, "they seem to be enjoying the coconut you chopped up for them, Halim."

The two baby orangutans are pulling apart pieces of coconut, chomping away like they haven't seen food for a while.

Just then Uncle Farhan returns carrying what look like two wooden chicken cages. He dumps them on the floor, says something to Halim and stomps out.

"My father said, we need to secure babies until we get them to Uncle Angga. He also said air room out, and then come to breakfast."

Guess he doesn't appreciate that these babies don't use bathrooms.

Something tells me this mealtime won't be as pleasant as last night.

20. Morning Plans

I get up to follow the guys to breakfast, but Stowe reminds me we need to brush our teeth.

"It's not like we have dragon mouth. We never even went to sleep."

My cousin gives me an eye roll. The girl is obsessed with good dental hygiene.

"Zap the water before you rinse," I say handing her the laser-sterilizer. "And change your shirt unless you want that honey-crusted shoulder to attract every bug in the rain forest."

With clean teeth, and Stowe in a bright blue t-shirt with a snow-capped landscape, we join the family breakfast. I didn't mind the delay in facing Uncle Farhan again. Hope he hasn't had time to think more about our nighttime adventure.

Everyone is already seated around the table. "Come try some *buburayam,* our traditional breakfast." Rafi has this amused look on his face, like he knows what Americans are used to eating. It would be annoying, except he may be trying to direct the conversation away from the orangutans.

Aunt Gita sets a bowl in front of each of us.

"Thank you. This smells good," Stowe says, but without the enthusiasm of the night before.

Must be the chicken shredded on top of the rice. This seems to be a theme.

Not the time to be rude, so we both smile and struggle through eating most of what's in front of us. I notice Stowe finds a way to bury the chicken at the bottom of the bowl.

Food is the least of our worries. "Rafi, are you going to call Angga to tell him what's happened, and figure out where we should meet them?"

"Or you could call Ariella," he says, staring right back at me. The standoff doesn't last long as Uncle Farhan's phone rings.

"*Halo* Angga." We understand the greeting, but after that we can only imagine the worst. Then Farhan thrusts the phone at Rafi.

"*Halo Ayah.*" Rafi does a lot of nodding, which his father can't see, and there are quite a few "*Iyas.*" I'm guessing that means yes. Finally Rafi says "*Sampaijumpalagi,*" and hangs up.

"What did he say?" Stowe asks, her body hunched up like she expects to be yelled at.

"My dad was pretty angry with us for sneaking out last night, but he said what is done is done. Now we need to get the babies to him as soon as possible. He, Ariella, and Bella are two or three hours from Sukadana. They will meet us at beach. Whoever gets there first is to text the other."

"And Ariella didn't want to talk to us?" Stowe wrinkles her brow and looks at me.

"No," Rafi said. "But I heard her tell Angga to pass on message that her grandchildren follow directions this time."

"We'll hear about it later," I say to Stowe, as we cross the hall and gather up our things. Rafi and Halim join us to pick up the cages with the babies.

"These cages not as heavy as the other ones," Halim says to Stowe, as we approach the HeliBoaJee. Then he turns to us. "Guys, sorry, my dad says I cannot go with you."

"Bummer," Stowe blurts out. "Without you last night, we wouldn't have made it."

All I can do is nod.

Halim puts down the cage, and deflects our disappointment as he pulls a t-shirt out of his pocket and throws it at me. "My old soccer shirt. Too tight. Figure no one in States have one. Don't worry, it was washed."

"We'll miss you," I tell our new friend. Hope we don't miss him too much.

My worries are interrupted as Gita comes running out carrying a pointy straw hat for Stowe. She says a few words, and looks at Rafi.

"My aunt says you should wear this, so you don't get sunburned when we get to Sukadana."

"I love it. This covers my ears. Much better than that old baseball hat." Stowe says as she balances it on her head. Then she whispers something to Rafi, and he answers into her ear. Not sure what's so secret.

"It's beautiful. *Terimakasih*," Stowe says, giving Aunt Gita and Hana big hugs.

Guess he gave Stowe the word for thank you.

I shake hands with Uncle Farhan, and wave to Hana and Aunt Gita. "*T-e-r--i-m-a k-a-s-i-h*—thanks," I say, hoping I used that right.

The family walks over to the HeliBoaJee with us. Stowe gestures for everyone to wait a minute as she goes into our vehicle to get something.

"Here," she says to Hana and Halim, handing them a few candy bars. "Sorry we don't have anything else to share." The kids get big grins on their faces. Who doesn't love a sweet? They can't appreciate how much Stowe loves her chocolate.

"Before we leave, I need a picture of the Rezaputra family," Stowe announces, pulling out her camera. "Rafi, you get in there with everyone." She snaps a few shots, gives one more round of hugs and then we're off.

"*Selamatjalan*," we call out.

Uncle Farhan waves and yells one more command.

We look at Rafi.

He said, "Remember, you go straight to Sukadana."

As we lift off in the direction of the rain forest we notice a small helicopter parked at the far end of the farm, its blades starting to whirl.

21. SUKADANA

"Why would a helicopter be parked so close to the farm?" I ask Rafi.

"Good question," he mutters, peering through binoculars. "No markings on it, so not a rescue helicopter. People around here do not own whirly birds."

"So who do you think it is?" No one pays attention to my leg. I guess everyone knows my distress signal by now.

Rafi just shrugs and shakes his head.

"Could it be the loggers? Have they been tracking us?" Stowe's speaking a little too fast. Never a good sign when she sounds nervous.

"Doubt it. They travel by foot a lot of time. When they leave the forest they are lucky if they have a battered pick-up truck, or some little boat. No way they would have helicopter." Rafi's conclusion makes sense to me.

"Loggers could have contacted traffickers, who will sell orangutan babies."

Unfortunately that thought also makes sense.

"Hope the 'copter people didn't hear Uncle Farhan tell us to go straight to Sukadana." I point back at the unmarked vehicle. "They're keeping their distance for now, but they're tracking us."

"Could we use the invisible shield like we did on the river?"

"Good thought, Stowe, but the blades would shear it. I'm worried they may try and force us down. Let's just hope the HeliBoaJee is faster than their aircraft. It is designed for speed. Let's try and outrun them. Rafi, any suggestions on a route?"

"Sukadana is north of here. If we have enough fuel, start flying east, do a loop around and head west. Then head to beach."

"Okay, point the way." I sure hope Rafi knows what he's doing. We can't afford to get lost.

I veer east, pushing the HeliBoaJee hard. Glancing back, I can see that we haven't quite shaken them yet. "It does look like they're having a hard time keeping up." Sure hope so.

"Do a 180, *now*," Rafi commands.

A couple of quick maneuvers and we're going back the other way.

"Looks like you lost them," Stowe says, peering through her binoculars.

"I hope you're right. Would be pretty hard for an ordinary helicopter to pull off that turn."

"Uncle Farhan said head north to Sukadana when we reach the border of the burned-out forest," Rafi says, pointing at the charred landscape below.

"What happened down there?" Stowe gasped.

"I know, looks terrible," Rafi said shaking his head. "Remember I told you how farmers drain the peat swamp? It dries up and becomes flammable. A few years ago fires were so bad we wore masks, just to be able to breathe."

Stowe's eyebrows scrunch up and her teeth clench. "And what happens to the animals when there's a fire?"

"Nothing good. A lot of them burn up. If they escape, they need to find new homes."

"And that can get them in other trouble," Stowe pipes in.

"Exactly. Preventing habitat loss is what my father care about most."

While they're busy chatting about landscape abuse, I've piloted us to our destination.

Stowe peers down below at the crescent-shaped beach. "It's even more beautiful than I remembered."

Squinting, I make out a small object some distance behind us. "Uh-oh. Looks like we haven't lost our tail."

"Rafi, call Angga and see how far they are from here."

Our fearless guide gets his father on the phone. Nice to have a conversation when we're not in trouble.

"He and Ariella still an hour away. Their boat only has one speed." Rafi reminds us.

"My dad said find a place to land and stay out of sight."

"You told him we were being followed?" Stowe asks.

Does she still think we should handle this ourselves?

"I had to tell him. We can't let him be surprised."

As we approach the beach, I see a stand of trees that has created a sheltered area. "We can land over there," I point. "Once we're on the ground, I'll pull the invisible shield over the HeliBoaJee before those guys can figure out where we've landed. But we have to move fast."

Stowe and Rafi nod in agreement.

"Here we go." I set the HeliBoaJee down in the tight grove, and hit the command for the covering to emerge and surround us.

"There's one problem," I mumble. "The shield was designed for boat mode. The rotors are still sticking out."

We look at each other, but it's too late to do anything about it now. We hear the whirl of a helicopter in the distance. It flies right overhead and keeps going.

"Maybe with the body of the HeliBoaJee invisible, the traffickers didn't see us?" Stowe wonders out loud.

"Let's hope. Rafi, text your dad and tell him where we are."

We sit inside for quite a while. It's getting hot, but we don't dare turn on any motor to give away our position.

The babies have been napping. The motion of the Heli-BoaJee must have rocked them to sleep. But they are up now, and not happy.

Rafi turns to our caged friends. "We have to quiet them down."

Stowe starts rummaging around. "We didn't take the honey Halim used earlier, and there's no other food."

"I have an idea. Wheaton, can I get out of here for few minutes without damaging our cover?" Rafi asks.

"Why?" I don't like the idea of rainforest boy getting caught again. Once was enough for me.

"There's a rambutan tree over there," he points. "And looks like fruit has come in. If I can pick a few, our little friends will be happy."

I lift the cover enough for Rafi to slip out the door and down the rope ladder to the ground.

Stowe and I take the babies out of their cages, hoping that by holding them we can quiet them down until Rafi gets back.

I hold Buddi. The sides of his mouth are pulled back showing his teeth. "Stowe, he looks so scared."

"Yeah. Poor sweet babies. Just stroke his back and hold him against you," she says, demonstrating with her little fella.

I follow instructions and before long Buddi has wrapped his very long arms around my shoulders and his legs around my waist, his head burrowing into my chest. He's so quiet I can almost hear his heart beating.

"He doesn't smell bad, maybe even a little like a lemon or something," I say to Stowe. "I guess the stink back at the Rezaputra farm was from the little guys peeing."

We turn our attention to Rafi who has climbed the rambutan tree, yanked off half a dozen red fruits, and shoved them in his pocket. He clambers up our ladder and back on board. We pull the invisible curtain shut again.

"Here you go," Rafi says, as he slices open the rambutan skins and pops out the edible round white fruits. He slits them open and gives each baby a few pieces.

The little orangutans pick up what's been offered and roll the fruits around in their hands. Buddi sniffs at his half, and the other orangutan rubs his fingers across the cut end and licks them.

Rafi smiles. "This is a new fruit for them. There is a seed in the middle. Watch what they do."

After a little more investigation Buddi takes a bite and spits the seed in Rafi's direction. His friend follows suit.

Our entertainment is interrupted by a couple of voices. I turn to Rafi. "Is that your dad?"

Rafi shakes his head and puts his finger to his lips.

The conversation is getting louder by the second. Whoever they are must be getting closer. Rafi looks as white as Stowe. If I had a mirror, I'm sure my face wouldn't look any different.

As the talking gets closer I can feel Buddi shaking in my arms. I wonder if he can sense that these are unfriendly voices.

"Please don't start crying now," I whisper, stroking his back.

I give him another rambutan fruit. He snaps it from my hand and nips me in the process. The pain is a distraction, but I manage to keep it to myself.

The voices are so close to us now that we can hear a conversation. The tone is ugly.

All I can think is, "Please stay on the other side of the trees. Please don't run into us because you can't see us."

It seems like forever, but then we hear the footsteps retreat.

"That was close," Rafi says. "We were right, those are traffickers." To my surprise, he laughs.

"What are we missing? Did they tell a joke or something?"

"No. But they saw the rotor. I guess it looked hooked to a tree. One of them said must be from a helicopter accident. He wondered about the rest of it!"

Rafi's phone buzzes. "*Halo Ayah.*" He smiles and gives us a nod. This conversation is longer than the previous one.

When he hangs up he's still smiling.

"Ariella and my dad are on the beach. I told him about our visitors, and where we are. He will look for rotor in tree. They should be here very soon."

We stay put, and before long we hear another set of footsteps.

22. Poachers Return

Not sure which of us is more relieved, as Angga approaches the grove where we are hiding. I hit a few keystrokes and our invisible shield retracts.

Angga steps back and sees the whole HeliBoaJee.

I throw open the door and the three of us crowd at the entrance.

"Ha, quite a trick," he says.

Stowe clambers down the stairs. "We are so happy to see you." She gives Angga a big hug, but then looks around. "Where's Ariella?"

"On my boat. Remember, Bella is with us."

"The traffickers are nearby. They visited a little while ago, but did not see us," Rafi says, giving me a big pat on the back.

"Should we bring out the babies?" I ask.

Angga looks around, and then starts speaking softly. "No, let me come up. You kids move back inside too. These guys could return."

With all of us on board, Angga takes a look at our two charges.

"They in good health. Not been in captivity long."

"We've fed them durian and rambutan fruits. And a little bit of honey," Stowe reports.

Stowe shows Angga which of the two is Buddi, and then asks, "What happens to our babies next?"

"The answer easy for Buddi," Angga tells us. "We reunite him with his mother in a few minutes. We get them both to the IAR facility until Bella is well. Then the pair returned to forest."

"*Yes!*" Stowe pumps her fist. "And do you know who our other little guy belongs to?"

"No." Angga shakes his head. "If we do not find his mother, he be raised at the orphanage. The scientists there are wonderful. He join a group of motherless orangutans, and the keepers introduce him to the foods of the forest. They teach him to take care of himself, and one day he become big and strong enough to be released into the wild."

At that moment Angga's phone buzzes. He listens for a while, his eyes squinting and his mouth getting tight. "What I was afraid of. Be there in few minutes," he tells the caller.

"That was Ariella. She says your visitors watching me, and they are coming this way."

"What do we do now?" We aren't going to escape their notice twice.

"How fast can you convert this thing to jeep? And can you shield it again?" Angga asks. Can't decide if he believes in me or not.

"I can make the Jeep invisible in a minute or so, but our wheels will show. Otherwise we won't be able to move."

"Better than nothing. Get down to edge of water, and hope traffickers don't realize what is happening. Or at least cannot catch us." Angga's taking charge. It's kind of a relief.

"And what happens then? Those guys can get aggressive." Rafi's speaking from experience. An experience I'm guessing he won't be sharing with his father.

"Transfer Bella to the HeliBoaJee, and you three take the orangutans to IAR. After you deliver them, fly back here.

"Not much time. Wheaton, get going," Angga commands.

While I retract the rotors and landing skids, and pop out our wheels, Angga gives Ariella a call. He asks her to help Bella out of the boat to meet us.

With the shield secure around our Jeep, I pull out of the grove.

We see the chase helicopter parked pretty close by.

"Uh-oh. Here come the bad guys." Stowe points about 50 yards/meters, whatever, from us. They're on foot. No convertible copter for them.

We see two men in cargo pants and green t-shirts that look like they've been through the wash one too many times. And they're wearing baseball hats with some sort of insignia. Can't make it out, but sure don't want to get any closer. These are the associates of the guys who shot Bella.

"Hold on to those cages. We're going to make tracks." Our wheels spin for a few seconds but then, with sand flying everywhere, we leave the traffickers in the dust.

Rafi looks back and starts cracking up. "Did you see the look on their faces?"

"Odds are they've never seen wheels moving with nothing on top." I chuckle and give Rafi a high-five.

While we're crossing the beach to the water's edge, we see Ariella wading into the water from Angga's boat, holding Bella as they move toward shore.

"Orangutans do not know how to swim," Angga tells us. "Bella is a large female, maybe 55 kg—"

"Around 121 pounds," Stowe interrupts.

That Stowe, still showing off her mathematical skills.

"—but in water Ariella can hold her."

As we reach the point where the sand meets the water I slam on the brakes.

"You're such a hot shot," Stowe says, giving me a nudge.

"We need to hurry." Angga glances back. The traffickers, still on foot, are heading down the beach in our direction. "Rafi, take Bella from Ariella and get mother orangutan into the HeliBoaJee. Wheaton, when they are on board, convert back into Heli mode and get out of here."

Rafi jumps out of the Jeep and runs to relieve Ariella of her burden.

"Stowe, pick up Buddi and hold him at the door," I say, as I retract our shield in preparation for take-off.

As soon as Stowe gets Buddi in Bella's line of sight, the mother orangutan breaks loose from Rafi's grasp and races into the HeliBoaJee with Rafi right behind her.

"No stopping mama." Stowe slides backwards, releasing the baby into his mother's frantic arms.

"Get going, kids," Angga yells. "Call when you get to IAR."

The traffickers are so close that I can make out the ivory tusk images on their hats. We've got to get out of here.

"Rafi, pull the door shut." I convert us back to Heli mode in record time.

"Hold on, lifting off now," I yell over the noise of the rotor.

Down below we see Ariella with her largest telephoto lens pointed at the two men. This time she's photographing real criminals.

"Uh-oh," Stowe says, peering down at the men. "Looks like they're getting ready to charge Ariella. Bet they don't want their pictures taken."

"I think you're right," I say. "Hold on, we're making a little detour before heading to the IAR." I pilot our copter a little further up in the sky, rotate around and dive bomb the ivory tusk boys.

"Way to go, Wheaton!" Stowe yells. "Look at those suckers duck for cover."

We hover above, close enough to the ground to insure that the traffickers don't get up. Angga is striding toward them carrying something bulky. "What's he got there?"

Rafi smiles. "Ha. I think I know what my father's doing."

Angga approaches, staying low to the ground. The guys are trying to slither away.

"Wonder what they're afraid of? It's not like they captured Buddi. Even if that was their plan, Angga can't prove it." I don't understand what's going on here.

"Who knows," Rafi says, "they could have critically endangered animals in chopper already. Or they may recognize my dad from other times they were in trouble."

"We aren't going to let them escape," I say, tilting the HeliBoaJee to keep them contained. As we hover above, Angga hoists a fishing net over one of the men. Even from up here, we can see that it's heavy. The harder the guy twists the more he gets tangled up. The other trafficker is still trying to escape so I bring us down a few feet more. He curls in a ball, making it really easy for Angga to cover him with a second net. Angga looks in our directions, gives us a nod, and signals for us to go.

"Check it out," Stowe whoops. "Look at those dudes wriggle. They look like fish pulled onto land."

Rafi takes over as navigator. "This will be short trip," he says, providing me with the coordinates for our destination.

Bella is holding Buddi tight.

"How do you say friend in Indonesian?" Stowe asks Rafi.

"Teman."

Stowe picks up the other orangutan baby and strokes his cheek. "Teman, we are taking you to a new home."

23. Special Delivery

After about fifteen minutes, Rafi points to a small clearing below.

"That's it? Pretty small." I say.

"Wait until you see the whole facility. It is 150 hectares. A lot in forest and peat swamp."

Stowe pipes up. "Swamp? Watch where we land."

"Gee, thanks, Stowe." Enough already.

I set the HeliBoaJee down close to the main building, and the three of us jump out. A woman and a couple of men greet us, dressed in green scrubs and masks.

"_Halo_. Angga has let us know you were coming. I am Syifa, the veterinarian here at IAR." The woman is younger than our mothers and no taller than Stowe. Her large brown eyes and large smiling jaw make us feel comfortable with the first hello.

"Please meet Bintang and Fariz, my assistants." They give us gloves, and then we all shake hands.

"Come aboard and meet your new guests." I point the way, and we all climb into the HeliBoaJee to see the orangutans.

"This is Teman," Stowe says, as she lifts the little orphan from his cage and hands him to Syifa. "And there are Bella and Buddi."

Syifa carries Teman out of the HeliBoaJee. Bintang pulls some durian out of a bag and climbs down the ladder. Buddi holds tight to Bella as she follows the scent of her favorite food. Fariz comes out last, to make sure there's no backtracking.

All of us walk to a white building nearby. When we get there, Syifa stops. "Time to say goodbye. We need to quarantine these animals, to make sure they have not contracted diseases during their sad journey."

"Wait while I take a few photos before we leave them."

As Stowe walks around, taking pictures from every angle, the orangutans turn, never taking their eyes off her.

"They like you," Syifa says with a smile.

"I can't believe this is it. We'll never see Teman and Buddi again." Stowe wipes a tear from the corner of her eye.

"I understand," the vet says to us. "We are all very attached to orphans."

When the photo-shoot is finished, we watch the caregivers escort our primate friends into their new home. "We'll miss you," Stowe calls after them. "He's so little. I hope he'll be okay."

The orangutans turn to look at us one last time, and it almost seems like Teman is waving.

We both know this is the best thing for Teman, but after holding these babies, it's hard to see them being taken away.

"Bintang and Fariz will watch over them," Syifa assures us.

"How long will Bella and Buddi have to stay here?" Stowe asks.

"That depends how long Bella takes to heal, and if either she or Buddi has health issues. If they are well, they may be ready to leave in two months."

"And Teman? What will become of him?" Stowe's eyes are big and watery.

"Come with me," Syifa says, pointing to a wooded path. "When we are sure Teman is healthy, he will come here, to orangutan preschool."

We peer into an enclosed area and see five little orangutans all sitting in a wheelbarrow together. There are climbing areas, and all kinds of trees with the fruits orangutans like. "We want young orphans to explore the environment, but in a protected space," Syifa explains. "They can build nests and sleep outside. But some feel more secure coming down at night to sleep in cages.

"As they get older they move to Baby School, then Forest School and finally Pre-release Island. Teman will go through all these phases until he is strong enough to be released."

"And you're sure he'll be ok?" Stowe asks, her eyes wide with worry.

"In nature there are no guarantees. Our goal is to give these orphans best chance for success in the wild."

Stowe pulls a piece of paper and pen from her pack. "Here is my contact information. Could you text or email updates on Teman's progress?"

"And Buddi and Bella," I add.

"Of course." Syifa smiles. She adds, "Rafi, call your father. It is almost 3:00 PM. You three must get back to Sukadana."

Stowe can't resist taking a few more pictures of the orphans, and then we head to the HeliBoaJee.

"*Terimakasih*," Syifa says. "You have given these animals a chance at survival."

After saying our goodbyes, we take one last Heli trip together.

This time when we pull above the treetops it feels different. The canopy is no longer a screen hiding the orangutans from our sight, but a warm blanket sheltering them in their new home.

The idea of a warm, cozy blanket reminds me of how tired I am. But it's not time for a nap quite yet.

Of course, Stowe can keep conversation going no matter how sleepy she is. "Can't believe we'll be home soon. It feels like we've been on another planet."

"Yeah, but I have to come back to earth and finish a robotics project I'm working on. Maybe someday I can come up with a robot to scout the rain forest for poachers."

"If anyone could invent something like that, it would be you, Wheaton," Rafi says. "I go back to school in a few days. But I have some new ideas for my paintings."

"And I have a mountain of school work to tackle. I think there's a creative writing assignment waiting for me. Maybe I'll write about this adventure. Then I can choose the ending." Stowe smiles and gives her arms a big stretch.

24. TIME TO SAY GOODBYE

W e're back at Sukadana. Ariella and Angga are wait-ing for us, the traffickers nowhere in sight.

Stowe bounds off the HeliBoaJee first and heads straight for Angga. "What happened to the traffickers? Did they get away?" My cousin is still revved up.

"Slow down," Angga says, and smiles. "I'll answer all your questions.

"After trapping our 'friends' in the fishing net, I was able to handcuff them. We went and examined their helicop-ter."

"Were there other animals in there?" Stowe asks.

"No, but it was loaded with cages, stun guns and all the tools of their trade. That's when I called for backup."

Ariella jumps into the conversation. "Angga's associ-ates were here within 30 minutes of the call. They took the men away and flew that unmarked helicopter to someplace where they can analyze it and its contents. They'll be able to tell what kinds of animals the traffickers have been transporting. Those guys could be put away for a long time. You kids have done more than just rescue these two orangutans. You may have saved a lot of other endangered animals."

Ariella's praise feels pretty good, but the story doesn't seem quite finished.

"And the loggers turned poachers?" I ask. "They get away with what they did?"

"Maybe not," Angga says. "You gave me the coordinates of their camp. It should not be too hard to catch them."

When we flew over here, I thought this would be straightforward. Find a baby orangutan, return it to its mother, and fly home. I guess there's a lot more to ResQ than just a simple rescue.

Ariella looks at Stowe and me. "I think we need to be heading out."

Stowe folds her hands together and looks at Ariella with a pleading face. "Oh, not yet. We may never be on a beach in Borneo again. Please let us go for a swim."

Ariella looks at her watch and then at Rafi's dad. "There are another ninety minutes until sunset. I think we can give the kids a little time for some fun. They've earned it."

Angga agrees. "Go jump in water. We will watch you from the beach."

"Please don't swim out too far. I think we've had enough excitement for one trip," Ariella says, flashing us a big smile.

The three of us take turns going up into the HeliBoaJee to get changed.

"Last one in is a rotten egg," Stowe yells as she charges down the beach. At least she didn't say a poached egg.

For a moment I forget we're in the tropics and brace myself. But as we plunge in, the warmth is welcoming, like the world's biggest bathtub.

We splash around, laughing and kicking the water high in the air. And then the three of us float on our backs, our feet touching as we form a star. The sun is still so bright, we have to close our eyes.

"Glad I got to come with you guys," Rafi says.

"We couldn't have been successful without you," I tell our friend.

Stowe pipes in. "Our two families made a great team. Maybe we'll get to work together again someday."

We've been floating for a while, and since we missed a lot of sleep, we're getting pretty relaxed. But then we hear our grandmother calling. "Come on out, ResQ team. Time to go."

Ariella and Angga meet us at the water's edge.

"Wait a minute," Stowe requests. She races back to the HeliBoaJee and returns wearing the hat Aunt Gita gave her.

"Please take our picture before we go," Stowe says grabbing Rafi's hand and mine.

"Okay, on count of three say DURIAN." Ariella snaps a bunch of pictures, and promises to send the best ones to Rafi and Angga.

"Come back when you get that scouting robot finished," Rafi says to me.

There's a final handshake and some hugs (Ariella and Stowe, not me). Then the forest ranger and his son depart.

Ariella puts her arms around the two of us, as we watch the sun dip beneath the waves. Looks like Borneo is saying goodbye to us.

EPILOGUE

July 4

At home

Hoboken, New Jersey

I just got off the phone with Stowe. She and her family are going hiking in Maine. They were going to come down for the fireworks, but decided they didn't want to deal with the holiday traffic. Ariella and I have gone on a few simpler rescues in the U.S., but Stowe didn't have time to come all the way down here and go with us. I need to solve that problem. Rescues without my cousin are a lot less fun.

Stowe told me she heard from Syifa at IAR. In June Bella and Buddi were released back into the wild. Wildlife ecologists are keeping an eye out for them when they're in the field – a couple of sightings and the pair looks good. Teman has gained weight, and is doing well at the orphanage. He's learning a lot, but Syifa said he will be with them until he's older. They want to be sure, when they release him, he's ready.

We both heard from Rafi. He sent a photo of his latest painting—Buddi reunited in Bella's arms. It's great, and got him into art school.

I'm back home with my family this summer, and plan to take a graduate school course in Crystal Chemistry in the fall. With only one course I'll still have time to spend helping Ariella with special projects for ResQ.

My grandmother bought an old building in Hoboken right near where my family lives, and she's getting it set up as ResQ headquarters. She's been hanging pictures Stowe took from our Borneo adventure.

Wonder where we'll be going next?

ACKNOWLEDGMENTS

This story and the characters are fictitious. My inspiration comes from the wonderful scientists and keepers at the Smithsonian's National Zoo and Conservation Biology Institute. The natural history described in this book is based upon fact as determined through the literature, and first hand accounting of people who know the orangutan and the environment in Borneo. Special thanks to Meredith Bastian, Curator of Primates for the National Zoo for her detailed reading of this manuscript. Thanks to Cam Webb who took the time to call me from Borneo and help me visualize this remarkable place. The Materials Research Institute at Penn State provided the inspiration for Wheaton's futuristic inventions. Thanks to Carlo Pantano and Edward Liszka for brainstorming with me, and helping me understand the underlying principles of the materials used in the story. Thanks to all the readers of this manuscript from its inception—especially the Writers4Kids of State College, my exceptional editor/publisher, Pendred Noyce, my husband Ira for all his encouragement, and Hudson Jeremy Pell-Gibson, together with whom the whole idea of ResQ started.

ABOUT THE AUTHOR

Eva Pell is a PhD biologist who has studied health and disease of plants. She was the Sr. Vice President for Research and Dean of the Graduate School at the Pennsylvania State University and was Under Secretary for Science at the Smithsonian Institution. She and her husband have three grandchildren, and this is her first book for kids.